SPLIT OPEN

A Novel

SPLIT OPEN

A Novel

GRETA LIND

– POND READS PRESS –
Saint Paul, Minnesota

Split Open © copyright 2021 by Greta Lind. All rights reserved. No part of this book may be reproduced in any form whatsoever, by photography or xerography or by any other means, by broadcast or transmission, by translation into any kind of language, nor by recording electronically or otherwise, without permission in writing from the author, except by a reviewer, who may quote brief passages in critical articles or reviews.

This is a work of fiction. Names, characters, places, and incidents are either the products of the author's imagination or are used in a fictitious manner, and any resemblance to actual persons, living or dead, businesses, events, or locales is purely coincidental.

Pond Reads is committed to turning interesting people into independent authors. In that spirit, we are proud to offer this book to our readers; however, the story, the experiences, and the words are the author's alone.

Edited by Kerry Stapley
Racial bias sensitivity read by Maresa Murray, PhD
Production editor: Hanna Kjeldbjerg
Author photo by: Laura Von Telthorst
Stock images by Unsplash.com

ISBN 13: 978-1-64343-825-2
Library of Congress Catalog Number: 2021907522
Printed in the United States of America
First Printing: 2021
25 24 23 22 21   5 4 3 2 1

Book design and typesetting by Athena Currier.
Typeset in Adobe Garamond Pro

Pond Reads Press
939 Seventh Street West
Saint Paul, MN 55102
(952) 829-8818
www.BeaversPondPress.com

To order, visit www.GretaLind.com. Reseller discounts available.

Contact Greta Lind at gretalind.com for speaking engagements, book club discussions, freelance writing projects, and interviews.

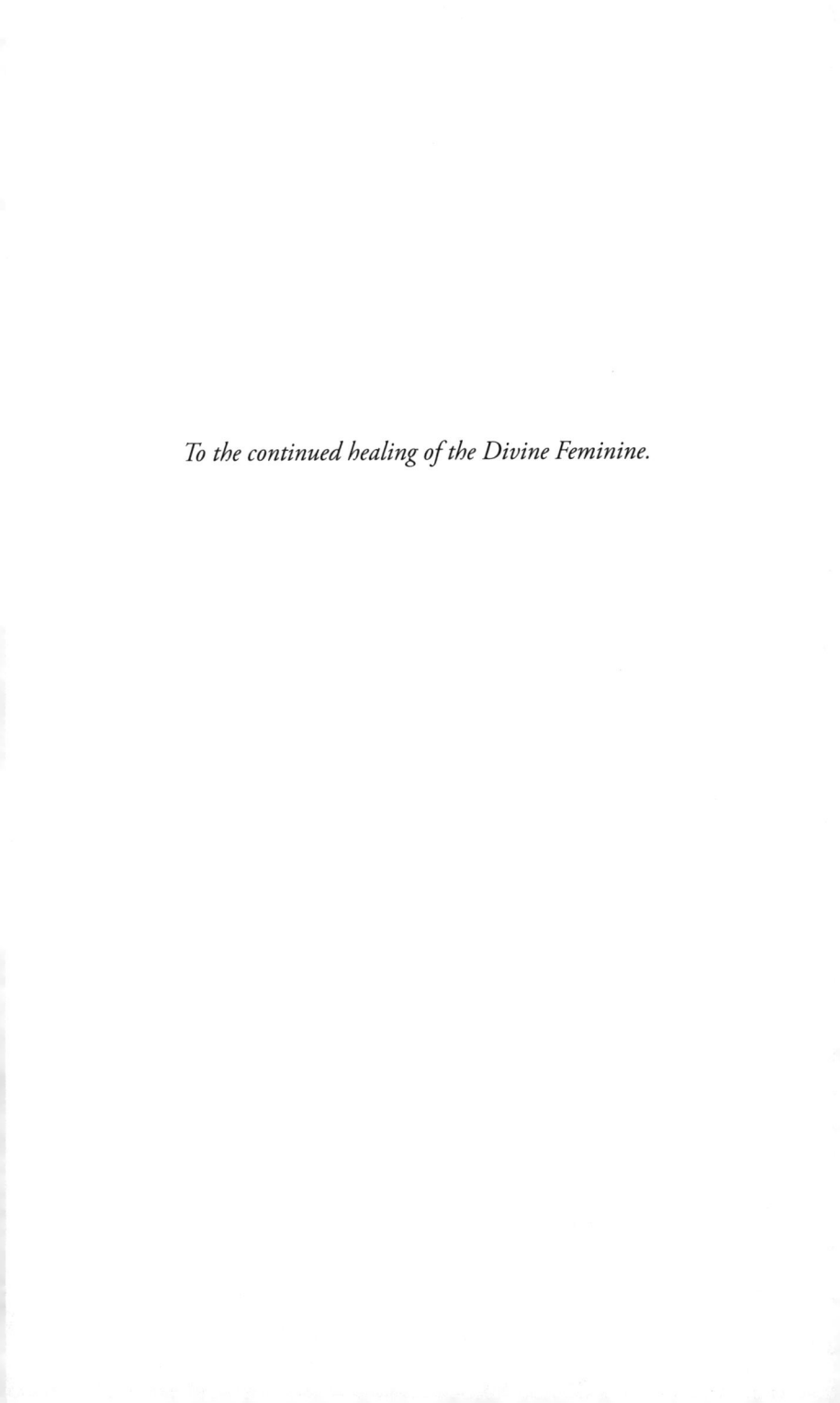

To the continued healing of the Divine Feminine.

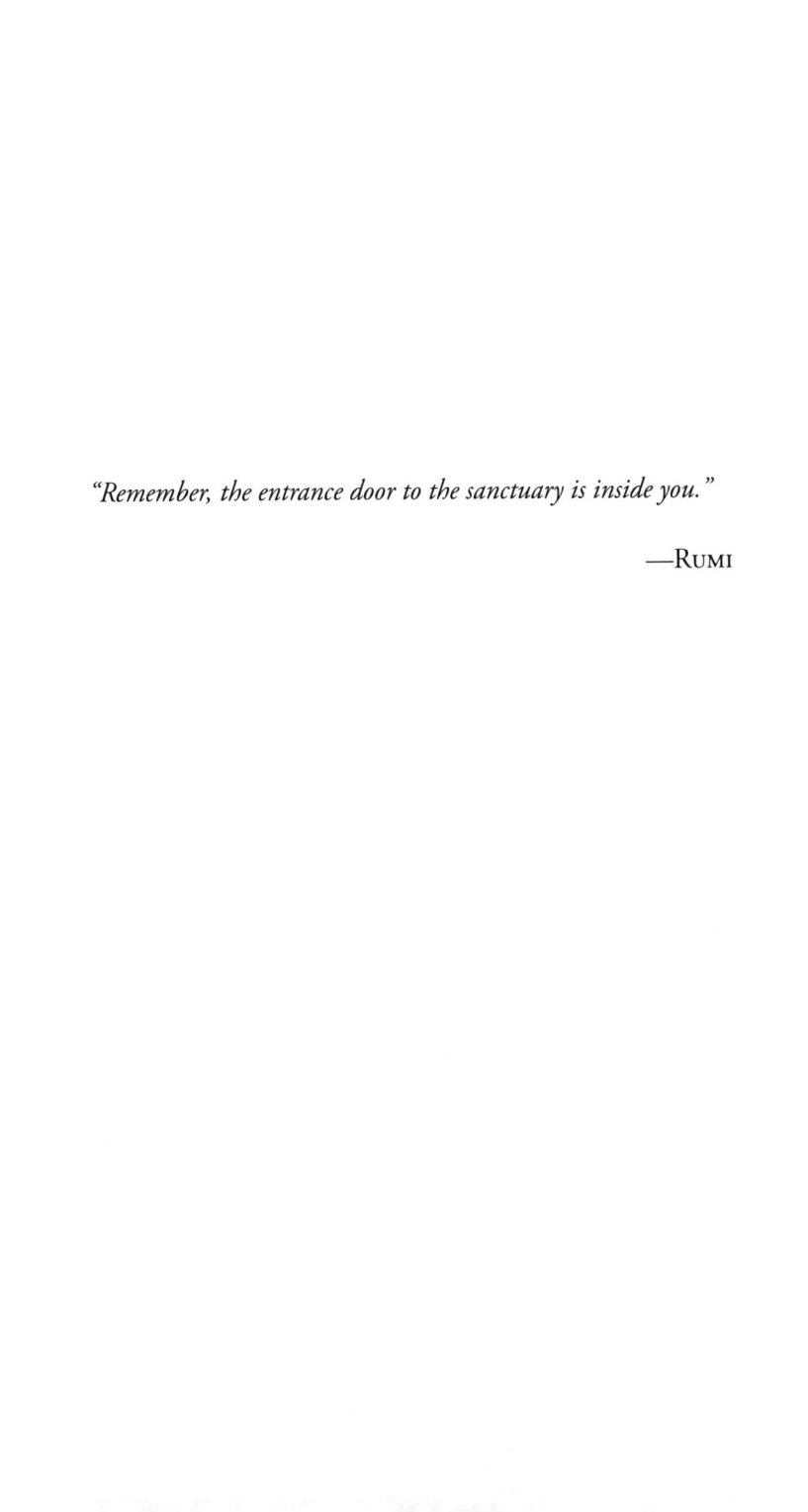

"Remember, the entrance door to the sanctuary is inside you."

—Rumi

YEAR ONE

LONGING

Kate

THE SUN IS SO BRIGHT IT ALMOST HURTS. I WANT TO GO HOME. Tired children chatter on the sidewalk. I feel a specific kind of post–field trip exhaustion in my bones. I lift hot hair off the back of my neck for relief.

The school bus finally pulls up. As we prepare to board, the bus driver steps off, saying she needs to grab a cup of coffee. It's past time to leave the Santa Barbara Mission and head back to Ojai. Coffee sounds good. Just a few more minutes . . .

A parent talks to me about volunteering. I half listen. There is a seamless moment when color begins to move gently behind her. As if I am one with the yellow, I simply say, "The bus is moving."

Then so am I. With the bus.

I push the door open, climb on, and sit in the driver's seat. I am at the top of a steep hill. Just below lies a busy intersection crowded with pedestrians. They don't see.

The bus is rolling...

I scan: large steering wheel, big windows, strange metal pedals. No emergency brake. Nothing to pull or push to stop the bus. It's picking up speed.

"Step on the brake!" A voice. Someone is running beside the bus.

I don't know which pedal—or what will happen. Nothing looks familiar. The intersection. They still don't see the bus. My foot lifts. I hold my breath.

My foot lands. The brake pedal. Everything stops.

I am frozen in the driver's seat. I turn to see the children and chaperones on the sidewalk, also still. The driver emerges, coffee in hand. Her face is ashen.

What almost happened...

We ride back home. Everyone is safe. Children whisper. I don't hear their words, only the whooshing inside my head.

Questions come over the next three days. Right now, there is only one: Who was that woman? Without fear or thought, she jumped on a runaway bus and stopped it.

Kate lays down her pen, turns out the light, and falls back to sleep.

)))

BED. HER HEART POUNDS. LIKE SLOGGING THROUGH MOLASSES, Kate pulls her awareness from a dreamworld, a party. She is disoriented.

It's light outside. How is it already morning? She turns over. David. Asleep. Like their marriage. And ever since she stopped that bus, something in Kate has felt oddly awake.

David's dark hair, chiseled face, and reclusive body language—even in bed—feel familiar. Reassuring, yet unsettling. Kate shakes him.

"I'm scared."

"What do you mean?" he mumbles.

"I don't know." Kate stares at the ceiling.

"I need more sleep. I was up late working." David pulls a pillow over his head.

"The boys have today off." Kate's heart sinks. "Remember?"

"Huh?"

"We talked about this. Several times. We're taking a hike and a picnic. As a family."

"I . . . There's no way," he mutters. "I have to work. You take them."

Kate's jaw tightens. Why is he so distant? "Come on, just for the morning?" she begs.

"I can't." He inches away. "Let me sleep."

"You were up playing computer hearts."

"What?"

"I saw you. When I went to the bathroom. At five in the morning." David rolls farther away. "Fine," she says.

Hearing PlayStation noises from the other room, Kate sits up. She looks at her watch. Why do the boys wake up so early on a day off? School mornings, they are sound asleep at this hour. Coffee . . .

Kate peeks in. "Hey! You know, you could've slept in."

"Mommy!" Ben hops up for a morning hug. His sun-kissed blond hair sticks out on one side, and his big brown eyes sparkle.

"Ben!" yells Peter. "I'm gonna get your guy!"

Ben rushes back to his seat, picking up the handheld control.

"Morning, Peter." Kate smiles at him.

"Hi, Mom." He barely looks up. "We can play today. There's no school."

"I know. It's fine. Just not all day."

"We know," he says, sounding like a teenager. He's far too young for that tone. Peter's thick hair looks darker. His facial features are becoming more defined.

"You guys want breakfast?" Kate asks.

"Later . . . Gotcha!" Peter shouts. Ben starts to cry.

"Go easy on him," she says. "Peter?" No response. "Peter!" Kate raises her voice.

"Huh?"

"He's three years younger than you. Remember that."

"Sorry. Okay." He looks up. Kind deep-dark eyes. "Hey, Ben, wanna pick the next game?" Ben's tears stop immediately. He runs to find his favorite music game.

"Being kind makes all the difference," Kate says gently. "Okay, hon?"

"Okay," Peter relents.

"I'll be in the kitchen."

"Then we're hiking?" Peter's eyes light up.

"Dad can't." Why does she have to say it? Disappoint her son. "But we can go."

"I thought Dad was coming." His face falls.

"Me too," Kate says. More to herself than to Peter.

"Forget it," he mumbles.

"Let's talk about it after breakfast."

"Ben's too slow." Peter stares at the screen. "It's only fun if Dad comes."

It is more fun when they're all together. "We'll have breakfast in a bit." Kate is thinking about coffee. "Pancakes? For special?"

Peter nods enthusiastically.

)))

Kate takes the jar of coffee beans from the cupboard and dumps a small amount into the grinder, pressing the On button. She pours coffee grounds into the filter. Filling the pot to the four-cup line, she adds water and turns on the machine.

No family hike today. She should have known. He used to be different.

She had fallen fast for David. It was their deep conversations. His talking. He was twenty years her senior and seemed wise. Worldly.

While having drinks with a small group of mutual friends, they went into their own little world. Just the two of them. Tunnel vision. When Kate looked up, almost everyone had left. She hadn't even noticed. David was eloquent, charming, and handsome. He told her she was special. Radiant. He made fun of the shape of her nose, but sweetly. Within the month, Kate was living in Los Angeles—a place she said she would never go—just to be near him.

The coffeemaker beeps. Kate pours a full mug and adds cream. She takes a sip. Hot and rich. The new dark beans were well worth the little extra cost.

And now, ten years later, joyful screams erupt from the next room. The last few years, Peter and Ben have discovered the fun they can have together. They are amazing. Smelling of sweat and spring. A depth of life has unfolded, opening Kate in ways she never imagined.

The coffee is hot in her hands. Kate brings it to the laundry room. Taking clothes from the dryer and adding them to the mound of clean-but-unfolded shirts and pants, she pauses. Underwear and socks sit in their own, ignored pile—to be avoided as long as possible. This looks like the scene of a normal housewife. It is not.

This is the unattended pile of her life.

Kate takes the items and carefully folds them. One by one. Her scream is silent. Invisible. Like she is. As she reaches for the whites, unable to procrastinate any longer, her breath quickens. With each tiny sock, while looking for its mate, panic creeps closer. This feeling is so familiar, like when she was young. Wetting the bed at six years old.

Was this how her mom felt in the household? It couldn't've been easy. They moved to an urban, religious commune in the early '70s, when Kate was three years old. Except for a few school friends—especially Nia—all Kate knew as a child was life in the fellowship.

The socks. She throws them back into the basket.

Peter and Ben are not so young anymore. She is still needed, but differently. And it will only continue to change. This ache. Her urge to move forward cowers in the face of her fear. How would she have time for anything more? Where would she find the energy? The confidence?

The bus. That was three days ago. Unable to integrate the experience, she finally wrote it down in the middle of the night.

There was something peculiar about that day. Kate felt oddly alert. When asked by a parent why she was on the field trip, she answered, "I'm here in case anything goes wrong." What a strange thing to say.

Had something within her intuitively known there would be an emergency? Was that why she was there? Or had it happened *because* she was there? Was it meant for her? As a test. And what—who—was that part of Kate that held such awareness? And acted with no fear . . .

Yelling. The boys. The beginning of an argument. She takes a last sip of coffee. Cold. Time to make pancakes. As Kate walks toward the kitchen, something hits the window, startling her. A tree branch. Huge gusts of wind blow outside. Kate watches the trees as they sway back and forth, bending easily. She stands transfixed.

How beautiful. What would it be like to move and flow so naturally while remaining strong and grounded? Kate feels a stab in her stomach. A longing for both the rising up and rooting deep. Ojai's trees feel reassuring, especially the old oaks, eucalyptus, and orange groves. There's something about them, especially at the "pink moment" of dusk with the Topatopa Mountains in the background.

For some reason, Kate was drawn to Ojai out of the blue when they lived in Los Angeles. She woke up one morning compelled to go. David agreed to go with her. Later, Kate discovered Ojai is believed to be a spiritual vortex. A fortunate place to live. The ideal small California valley town to raise a family in. A wonderful place to explore outdoors with the boys.

Kate walks into the family room. "Peter? Ben? Come help me make pancakes. Then we'll pack a lunch. We're hiking today."

)))

That night, the house is quiet. With the boys in bed and David writing in his office, Kate's mind returns to her earlier thoughts. Does David still find her attractive? He used to say such kind things. But she is no longer young and sweet. She's in her thirties, with stretch marks on her abdomen. And smile lines. She is a real live woman and mother, with real needs. Not a fantasy.

Kate feels a strange pull. She remembers the dream she'd had the night before. The party. It was nowhere she's ever been, yet it felt so real. And who was that woman in it? She was lovely, with dark blond hair and gray-blue eyes. She moved with ease. Irresistible and free.

Then Kate remembers; she told someone she was the luckiest woman there because she was no longer tied to a marriage. Two women whispered in the corner. They spoke of her husband's many betrayals and, finally, of her own. They said what she went through was unimaginable, more than anyone could bear. And she'd survived. She had come through the other side, not just intact. Transformed.

Who was this woman? What was her life like? How had her marriage dissolved? What about her children? (Does she have children?)

Who am I? Kate thinks. *Apart from David's wife. Apart from mother.*

Layers—years of buried feelings begin to peel open like an onion. It is too much. A huge gulf lies between what is conscious and what is not. Happiness has depended on keeping them separate.

And yet, Kate doesn't want her bus to run away downhill. She wants to sit in the driver's seat. But how?

Jennifer

As she stretches upward, Jennifer catches an accidental glimpse of herself, her appearance barely recognizable in the dusty mirror. Hair tossed, lips swollen, face fiery with sweat. The eyes of the woman reflecting back are exotic. Not her own.

"Come here," coos Andrew.

The voice, the ache, the pull. His embrace, warm and tight. Frightening. She must push fear out through the corners where it has begun to seep in. Not now. In Andrew's gaze, she is found. Gentle rocking, bodies humming, rhythm slowly . . . slowly growing. Goose bumps. She will feel this pleasure until it is time to go. That separation will fragment her, crush her. Bring sorrow and regret. But this . . . loving . . . is heaven-sent. Isn't it? Her body never lies. Every pore, her very core, pulses. Intoxicating pleasure. Her whole world splitting, opening, merging. Nothing separate.

Her children . . .

"Look at me."

His voice is low and assertive. Entrancing. She hadn't known she'd slipped away. His eyes. Dark hazel. His strong arms. How could she miss a single second? But holding this . . . being here . . . is hardly possible . . .

"Jennifer?" asks Andrew. "What's wrong?"

She is suddenly alert.

He is trying to understand. How could he ever know? His risk is nothing compared to hers. He has no family, no one counting on him. This thought cuts into her. She is everything she once judged so harshly. She feels more alive, and closer to death, than she ever has.

"I'm okay." She smiles. Betraying tears well up quickly. She cannot hold them. "I'm scared . . . I'll forget my children. I'm scared—"

"You won't." His voice. "I won't let you."

Jennifer is immediately repulsed, untrusting. Splintered. Ready to go.

"Promise?"

)))

JIMMY IS FULL OF ATTITUDE WHEN JENNIFER PICKS HIM UP from preschool. His darling pixie face is sour. Even his bright-blue eyes appear darkened.

"I'm sorry," she says. "We'll get juice at home."

"Want it now. Like every day. In the car." She is in no place to deal with her three-year-old's whining.

"Sometimes Mama's busy, then I come straight to get you." Jennifer steals a quick look back. "I love you."

"Can I watch TV?"

"A little. How was school? You have a good day?"

"It's okay."

"You eat your lunch?"

"Only juice and chips."

"If you eat your sandwich, it'll help you grow big." It's better not to push it. "You can watch *Sesame Street* till it's time to pick up Chloe. How about tomorrow I put in cashews instead?"

Silence.

"Love you too, Mama."

As she lifts Jimmy from his car seat, soft sweetness in her arms, Jennifer knows she is where she belongs. His warm little body melts into her, the perfect puzzle piece. Hardly able to put him down, she settles him onto the couch with hugs, kisses, and juice.

Home.

Was that her earlier? Was it real? Jennifer looks down. Her hands are shaking. She begins to pick up the house. Dirty clothes go in the hamper, dirty dishes in the dishwasher. But the shaking is deep. Jennifer walks back to the living room. She settles in next to Jimmy under the blanket. He leans into her. She breathes in the smell of sunshine, dirt, fun—and still a little bit baby.

She is safe.

Jennifer jolts upright. What time is it? She looks at her watch. Jimmy's breathing is steady. She scoops him up, along with her purse and keys, in one movement. Holding his heavy, sleeping body close, Jennifer manages to buckle Jimmy into his car seat without waking him.

She turns on the CD player. India.Arie. Jennifer sinks into a temporary haze. Maybe a cup of coffee after getting Chloe. The feeling of Jimmy is still in her arms. And she feels herself in Andrew's. How is she doing it? And how will she feel tonight when James comes home?

Chloe is on the swings with her best friend. They remind Jennifer of two characters in a fairy tale she once read when she was little. Chloe with her light, almost strawberry-blond hair and blue eyes. Lily with jet-black hair and fair complexion.

"Chloe!" Jennifer calls, waving. What a big girl. She has changed so much since she was Jimmy's age. This year especially—she's made a leap. "Hi, sweetie."

"Hey, Mom," Chloe says casually. Was it this year or last when she stopped saying *Mommy*? "Can Lily come play?"

"I guess it works for us. Let me talk to her mommy when she comes."

"She's over there." Chloe points.

"Okay, I'll go check with her."

The girls don't respond. They are busy talking about what color they'll paint their fingernails. Robotic, routine school drop-offs and pickups. Everyone appears the same. No one can tell about the life of another in these daily rituals.

Jennifer imagines what people see when they look at her. No one would ever guess. She must seem . . . how does she seem? Pleasant. Maybe kind. She is kind; that's never been a question.

She probably seems acceptable. And that, Jennifer feels, is no longer true.

What really goes on in the lives of other women? Could be anything. How many people carry secrets? What about larger, universal truths? Is this where we connect? Or is true connection buried in the fact that we cannot know the soul of another? Maybe secrets are necessary. What happens when our secrets are revealed? When the invisible is made visible?

"Mom!" Chloe yells. "She's leaving!"

Jennifer realizes she's been standing. Staring at nothing. She quickly walks over and talks with Lily's mom. What secrets does this woman hold? She seems overly mannered and perfect. There's no way that's the whole story. The playdate is on. Jennifer returns to the girls with the good news.

"Yay!" they scream. Chloe hugs Jennifer, handing over her backpack and lunch box.

"Come on, kids, I'll make you a snack," says Jennifer. "How about 'death-by-chocolate' brownies?"

In the lull of the car, with children buckled in, there's nothing to do but drive. How is it a person can feel both closer to and more disconnected from themselves at the same time? How can she want so many different things? Is there a deeper loyalty than our morals allow—a loyalty to self? At the level of soul?

Jennifer's mind drifts easily to the earlier lovemaking. So tender. She suddenly feels herself open, quickly. Wetness between her legs. What is happening to her?

The children are hungry. So is she. Jennifer preheats the oven. She smiles to herself as she takes her favorite brownie mix from the pantry shelf. She's sure Lily's mother would make them from scratch. Jennifer cracks an egg, watching its insides spill out. She feels herself falling into the bowl, sliding down the cool glass, and landing at the bottom. Adding oil and water to the mix, and stirring thoroughly, she dumps the batter into a glass pan. Brown lava. She can't resist scooping the bowl with her finger. They sure got the name right.

Jennifer cuts an apple. The girls chat about their playground dramas on the way to Chloe's room. Jimmy is content scribbling in his coloring book near her.

She marvels at the difference between her two children. Jimmy, always content to be close, hesitant to be apart. And Chloe, striving for independence from the very start. How she loves them both.

How old had Jennifer been the first time she made brownies herself? Chloe's age? When she learned to hold on to her house key, the most important thing. Then run home from school and lock the door. A box of brownie mix wasn't that much. She could save up her allowance. And her mom wasn't home for hours. Always working. Always tired. Jennifer longed for closeness that seemed to come only with the rare movie night. Popcorn and hot chocolate. A cozy blanket on the couch. Feeling her mother's big body next to hers.

The timer beeps.

"Brownies are ready!" Jennifer calls.

They are hot and perfect, just underbaked, as she pulls them from the oven.

Jennifer allows the girls to take their treats back to Chloe's room to eat in her fairy tent. It's just easier to say yes. She sits with Jimmy and helps him color awhile, welcoming the mindless activity. Melting chocolate penetrates.

"I want my train!"

"Oh yeah? Your birthday train?"

"Yeah!"

Good. This will give him hours of quiet playtime. She and Jimmy wash their hands and head for his room. Chloe has taped a Keep Out sign on her bedroom door in bright pink. Jennifer patiently helps lay out train tracks. She sinks into these moments with ease. Simplicity. She feels Jimmy's delight as they create a whole world on his floor.

Being with him. Being a real mom.

"Okay, sweetie, we did it!"

"It's our best!"

Jennifer laughs. "I think so too! And . . . I just realized I need to start dinner."

)))

As Jennifer chops onions, careful of her fingers and her tears, Lily's mom comes to pick her up. The playdate was more than successful. The girls are finally at an age where a friend in the house makes things easier. The right friend. They leave, and Jennifer's breath deepens. She looks in the refrigerator for an open bottle of wine. Thankfully, there is one.

James will be home soon.

The bottle, cold. The perfection of a single wineglass, fragile. How many has she broken in her life by being too rough? Too rushed? By not paying attention as she washed and dried the curved, delicate vessel. This glass fits perfectly in the palm of her hand, stem dropping between fingers. The pour is her favorite part. And the first sip.

Jennifer mixes chopped onion with other cut vegetables. She breaks an egg and adds ground turkey. Smushing it together, her hands cold to the bone from the meat, she remembers tomato sauce. She washes her hands, opens the can, and dumps it in. After molding meat loaf in the pan, Jennifer tops it off with ketchup and slides it into the oven.

She sections potatoes into fours and drops them carefully in water to boil. She watches the pieces land underwater. Drowning. A sip of wine lifts her.

Once the broccoli is cut and ready to steam, she can relax. She can relax into the fact that she has no idea where her life is going. Only wanting and reaching and fearing. Stabbing remorse. Then quick defiance.

Why shouldn't she have this? She didn't mean to; she wasn't seeking it out. She never thought she would be here. No one knew her capable. And as she thinks it, Jennifer knows that a person can change the very moment she does the impossible. It is then not only possible but already done.

Jennifer takes her glass into the bathroom. Just a look before he comes home. She needs to see what he will see. Sipping. Staring. Honey hair grown darker over the years. Messy. Tired, steel-blue eyes. Jennifer remembers the coffee she forgot to have. Her face looks somehow transparent. High cheekbones and paper-thin skin. Chapped lips. How swollen they were when she caught sight of herself earlier.

There is an unmistakable sound. A car. Turning off the bathroom light, Jennifer takes her glass to the kitchen. Heart pounding in her ears, she begins to steam the broccoli and checks the potatoes on the stove. Soft enough. She uses the strainer, dumps them into a large bowl, and grabs the masher.

"Hello!" James.

"I'm here." Somehow her voice sounds normal.

"Daddy!"

Jimmy comes bounding into the kitchen from his room and throws his arms around James's legs. Jennifer is still surprised by how handsome her husband is, especially in a suit. Exactly how he looked when they first met that night in the bar.

James sets his briefcase by the door.

"My boy."

"Wanna see my train?" Jimmy, so excited. "Do train like Mama!"

"Sure do. Where's your sister?"

"In here, Daddy!" Chloe cracks her door and peeks out. *Daddy?* Why has Jennifer alone graduated to *Mom*? "You can come in later. I'm making something."

"Top secret, huh?" James asks.

"Maybe!"

"Well. We are going to look at a very important train. All aboard!"

James bends down and over enough for his little boy to climb onto his back. He makes chug-a-chug-a-choo-choo sounds all the way to Jimmy's room.

Jennifer pulverizes the potatoes. She adds butter and salt. She then takes broccoli off the stove and checks the meat loaf. Almost done. She quickly sets the table and grabs a good bottle of red wine. An expensive one. Why not?

"Dinnertime!" she calls.

"Coming!"

The family. Together. In the kitchen.

"Okay if I open this?"

"Sure." James's smile, so charming. False picturesque promise. Perfect for a museum wall. "What the hell."

"Ooooh! Daddy!" Jimmy is delighted.

"You swore!" Chloe too.

"Oops. Sorry!"

Jennifer grabs two large red-wine glasses. James finds the opener and starts in on the bottle. Jennifer pours milk for the kids.

"Come on, cuties. Let's sit down." As they do, she dishes up their plates.

"What's this?" Chloe, so skeptical.

"You know what it is. Meat loaf. Mashed potatoes. And don't worry, your broccoli is soaked in butter." She looks up. "James, you mind grabbing the ketchup?" With the wine open, he is in mid-pour.

"Sure."

"No, I'll get it." Jennifer opens the refrigerator. "Here," she says to Chloe. "I'm sure this will make it much better."

Chloe pours a thick layer onto her meat loaf.

"Me too," says Jimmy.

James holds out her glass. "You look pretty."

A hairline crack of shame travels down her spine.

Jennifer blushes, her head hot. She accepts her wine. Silently, they toast. It's not fair. James will unexpectedly—rarely—hand her a tender moment. Then he withdraws. Possibility that never comes. Leaving her feeling more like shards of broken glass than like the whole stem in her hand.

Is it possible to sustain true intimacy within a marriage? Jennifer has tried to accept the emptiness—but finally felt she was dying inside. Alone. It's why she is reaching. For something to feel alive. She feels a chipping away at the marble of herself, like Michelangelo sculpting David, trying to free whoever wants to emerge.

The meal is fine. Surprisingly easy. There's conversation and the usual chaos. Then the children jump off their chairs looking for fun.

"Let's play Sorry!" Jimmy pleads.

"I'm doing my homework." Chloe is proud of her nightly assignments.

James drifts into the living room and turns on the television. It stings every time.

"Okay, sweetie, go get the game." Why is it only Jennifer who listens?

"I'm red!" Jimmy's favorite color at the moment.

"I'll be . . . yellow." Sunshine, brightness, purity. Jennifer would've chosen red if it were available. She moves a card or two around, just enough to avoid a meltdown. Jimmy loves playing and especially loves winning. Jennifer knows that as he gets older, she needs to help him learn how to lose too. An achingly important life lesson. But not tonight. Jimmy wins again.

"Wow! It's major bath time."

"Major not!" Jimmy giggles.

"Major so!" Jennifer grabs him playfully. "All aboard!"

Her body is bent and awaiting its passenger. Jimmy squeals and climbs on. Once in the bath, it's easy. It's the transition. Always, the transition.

With the children tucked in, Jennifer moves back to the kitchen. Tomorrow, she must make sure to have some quality time with Chloe. Where has this day gone? The dirty dishes aren't too overwhelming. Jennifer disappears into her thoughts. His hands . . . pressed hard against her as she lies in full surrender. Who could open her like this? An orchestra of longing and loving.

"I'll finish the dishes!" James shouts from the living room, startling Jennifer.

"No big deal. I'm almost done. I don't mind." It really is no big deal. She's lucky, after all. Isn't she? Anyone looking in would be envious. It all looks so good.

)))

Andrew meets her early today, as early as possible, full of heat and purring.

"You are so beautiful." His breath is warm, the heat melting her. He is different from anyone Jennifer has ever known. Strange, masculine, tall, muscular, capable. Smelling of herbs and earth, with the strong hands of a gardener. Jennifer loves to imagine him digging deep into dark, rich, wet soil.

Andrew's hands touch her face. They are large next to her delicate features. He moves them down her cheeks, bringing his fingers to her lips. She licks them. How is her mouth so transformed—her hunger so fierce—from a loving mother to this?

His hands move down her neck. Her breath entrains with his. He is molding her. Tending her. His hands almost encircle her waist.

"Jennifer," Andrew coos.

She runs her hands over his arms, feeling his strength. She wants to be taken.

"Who's your man?" His voice. The spell.

Andrew is the last man anyone would imagine her with. His face, weathered by the sun, looks older than his years. He's already twenty years older than she is, and oddly rugged. Unexpectedly sensual.

His power . . . overtaking her . . .

"You are."

He moves his fingers expertly. She is open . . . wanting. She can hardly remember the morning cereal or kids' clothes set out for school.

"I need—" Her voice falters.

"What?"

"I . . . need . . . please . . ."

"What do you need?" Andrew presses firmly.

"I need . . ." Rising. Lifting. Levitating. "You . . ." And in this moment, she is his. Completely. Everything white and silent.

Andrew scratches the bottoms of Jennifer's feet. "Stay with me," he says. "Who knows how to love you?" His eyes . . .

"You."

"Who takes care of you?" His voice takes her deeper. She can hardly think or hear. Andrew stills his movement. Tender teasing.

"Don't stop."

"Want more?" He has her.

"Yes. More."

Kate

"Mom! I'm starving!" Peter yells from the other room.

"I'm—" How is it so late? "I'll make something real quick!"

"Quesadillas?"

"Sure, honey. Is Ben with you?"

"Watching TV."

Great. She's finally involved in something for herself, and it means Ben has probably been in front of the television for hours. Suddenly, Kate realizes her own hunger. She hasn't eaten since breakfast. Is that possible? Writing all day?

As quesadillas cook, Kate slices whole red apples. She watches the knife cut through the core. What happens when parts are severed from the whole? Kate almost pierces her finger. She puts down the knife, places equal portions on plates, and clears the cutting board.

"Boys! Dinner's ready," Kate calls. "Hey, guys, come on! Ben, no more TV!"

Peter and Ben come running. They eat and talk, discussing the boys' favorite taboo subject, which, besides swearing, is crushes. They each admit to having one and are willing to reveal the girls' names. Last year, there were only giggles and secrets between the two. This year they want hard facts.

"My first crush," Kate answers, "was in first grade."

"What was his name?" Peter is curious.

"Jeff Pell. He used to chase me at recess. But he never caught me!"

"Who did you like in the second grade?"

"I don't remember. But in third grade, I had a huge crush on Johnny Porkel."

"Johnny Porkel!" They squeal with delight.

"And I was mean to him once. One day, my friends and I followed him home and called him '*Porcupine! Porcupine!*'"

"Did you make him cry?" sweet Ben asks. Her heart.

"Yes." Poor Johnny. Even as Kate was taunting him, she knew it was wrong. Did the fellowship friends she was with feel their trespass? Hers was especially bad because of her feelings for him.

"I really liked him a lot."

Kate remembers third grade well. The same year she met Nia. Thank goodness Nia has another research trip to Los Angeles planned. She'll be able to visit. Talking on the phone just isn't the same. And there's been so much to talk about.

After the bedtime routine of bath, stories, and a good long tucking in, Kate feels her body's exhaustion. Sometimes she is so tired by the end of the day, she can hardly stand. She longs to lie down. Surrender. Be tucked in. Have someone loving her, sweet to her, holding her tight.

A glass of wine sounds good. There's a bit left in an open bottle of red. After putting the empty bottle in the recycling bin, Kate takes a deep breath. The house is quiet. Hers. With David in Los Angeles, she is alone in her grown-up evening.

A bath . . .

Warm water offers its sweet caress. If not a lover, this is something at least. Kate reaches for her wine on the edge of the tub.

Why doesn't David hold her anymore? Do other husbands still touch their wives? What goes on in the lives and minds of other women? How much of it is really happening? And how much is thought, internal dialogue, and fantasy? No one truly knows another's experience. Yet there are rare moments when life opens and a kind of grace comes in. These moments inspire genuine intimacy and connection. Something sacred.

Kate remembers giving birth to Ben. During transition, it was time to shift from breathing deeply through increasingly intense contractions to beginning to push. Fear took over. She didn't know what was going to happen with the birth of another little one. She was scared to push him out. Scared of the pain and the work and the change. Kate lay in bed desperately looking at all the faces in the room thinking, *Who can take this from me?* David? Her sister, Rachel? The midwife?

There was a single moment when her fear crystallized. She had to do it. Reaching deep into her core, Kate started to push. She pushed that beloved baby out in ten minutes. Yet never forgot that moment. The desire to give in to fear. Fear of the unknown.

)))

Kate reaches out, laying a hand on David's shoulder. His breathing feels steady.

"You sleep okay?" she asks.

"Uh-huh. You?"

"Yeah. David?" Kate takes a deep breath and pulls his shoulder toward her. "When did you get home last night?"

"Around three."

"How come?" Her stomach tightens.

"You know." David rubs his eyes. "Work dinner."

"I waited up."

"I was too drunk to drive home," he sighs. "I had to sober up for a couple of hours."

"Was anyone else there?" Does she want to know?

"Where?"

"At dinner."

"No one you know." David rolls back the other way. Something isn't right. Hasn't felt right for a while.

"You want to take a walk this afternoon?" Kate tries to sound light. Cheerful.

"I can't," he groans. "I'm not a hundred percent." Heat rips through her body. He doesn't see. Isn't even looking. "What's wrong?" David asks.

"Nothing." She turns away.

"Well, it must be something. You're acting really strange."

She continues to move, bed no longer a comfort. "I need to get the boys up."

"I need more sleep." All he wants is to stay asleep.

)))

"Honey?" Kate sits on Peter's bed. "Time to get up. Want a quick bath?"

Peter grunts in protest. She strokes his cheek, so soft. Tears well up. She brushes them away. Leaning down, Kate buries her nose in Peter's hair.

"Time to get ready for school, love." She tousles his hair. "I'll start your bath."

The water warms her hand as she finds the perfect kid temperature. Kate carries her sleepy boy from bed to the bath.

"Dad back?" Peter mumbles.

"Yeah."

"What time did he come?"

"Late. He's still sleeping."

"Oh," Peter says quietly. "I wanted to ask him something."

"After school, you can." Her voice is calm. Unlike her stomach.

"He's never here." Her longing is one thing. But her son's?

"We'll make sure you get some time with him this weekend. Okay, honey bunch?" She must make sure that happens.

Peter nods.

"I love you, Peter." They smile at each other.

As she wakes Ben and helps the boys get ready for school, a memory flashes. Peter was a baby, around six months old, and Kate was very sick. Her body ached with fever—to the point of being unbearable. The only thing she could think of was the relief a hot bath would bring. David wouldn't get up with Peter. What was it he said once when she asked? That he was the one who worked and needed his sleep?

That day, he said he had to go work out. She begged him to stay. Then begged him to please come right home. The fever was consuming. Kate rarely made requests of his time, but she was desperate. He promised he would.

David came home five hours later carrying groceries. She was undone. Walking Peter up and down the hallway. Barely able to stand.

"Why didn't you come straight home? I needed you."

"I thought you'd want some things." He proudly showed off a gallon of ice cream, cans of soup, orange juice.

"I told you what I needed. Take Peter. I'm not okay." Far from okay. Kate took her sickness and the pit in her stomach to the bath. Hot tears merged with hot water. What could she have done? She had said so clearly what she needed. It hadn't mattered.

Her mom had told her that when she was little, Kate asked again and again for time with just their family. Apart from the household they lived in. Her mom brought the request to her dad, one of the fellowship's junior elders. He said no. Repeatedly. No.

Were things that different with David?

Feeling the water she hadn't realized was still running, Kate turns off the kitchen faucet and puts cereal bowls in the dishwasher.

"All right, boys. Here's your lunch, hon." She hands it to Peter. "For your backpack."

"Do I get gummies?" he asks.

"Yes."

"And me?" Ben's eyes are wide and hopeful.

"Yes, love. You get gummies. And a sandwich. And carrots. Eat those first, okay?" She grabs him for a quick squeeze.

"You're getting so big!" It seems only last week she could scoop him up with one arm. "Let's go!"

The drive brings on a daze. Kate turns on the radio.

"I want rap."

"Peter, why are you trying to grow up so fast?"

"Aah!" he whines. "I never get to do anything!"

Kate watches the trees as they pass a field of eucalyptus. How is it they don't split in two when the wind blows so hard? "Me neither," she whispers.

Jennifer

Jennifer sits in the morning sunlight, drinking a cup of coffee. Peace. With children at school and husband at work, she breathes in the solitude. Only her mind works its intrusive nature into this moment.

The split is deepening.

She has been seeing her lover for over a year. Who would've guessed the haphazard days would add up to such a significant amount of time? Every day seems a death and life reborn. Shaping her. Despite the lies, isn't this better than the shell she was in danger of becoming? At least she is living, feeling.

She feels the heat of the decision she must make coming closer. She can't go on like this. The duplicity is almost impossible to bear. So is either choice.

How can she not have this? His smell. His hands. His weight pressed against her. Dark and mysterious. Captivating.

She wants to be captured. The pull... His eyes, how they envelop her. He sees her. Wants her. Takes her. Now that she's had this, who would she be without it? Endless questions.

She picks up the phone. Dialing.

"Hello." Andrew's voice is low.

"Hi."

"I was hoping you'd call."

"I am," Jennifer whispers.

"When do I get to see you?" Wanting.

"Maybe now."

"Sooner the better."

"I need to take a quick shower." Jennifer wants to feel fresh.

"I'd like to see that."

She feels a rush. "Twenty minutes?"

"I'll be here."

"Okay."

"Bye, baby."

"Bye." She can hardly hear her own voice.

Jennifer's shower is fast and hot. Her flesh goose bumps with anticipation. She feels the ache. No one knows her like Andrew. She has caught him looking at her, seeing her in a way she doesn't know herself. She throws on a light, short skirt and tank top. Unencumbered. Her cheeks are bright pink in the mirror. She stares at herself.

)))

Andrew pulls her to him. He could break her. Their energy... Is it allowed to exist this way from being tucked away and hidden from the world?

"You look good," he says. His white hair is messy from the wind. He was probably up at dawn. Jennifer loves his hard work. His sweat. His sunbaked skin.

"So do you."

"You'll look better naked."

Jennifer laughs. "Well, then . . ."

He kisses her, their mouths melting together. Andrew strokes her hair. His hands move confidently, resting on her breasts, her back, her waist. She feels his body's urgency. He is impatient today. He unpeels her. His movements forceful, yet gentle. His body needs hers. He deserves her.

And she deserves her own, full surrender.

She has tried to stop. And has stopped. For months at a time. But her longing slowly pulls her back, past husband and children, and life—to him. And he is there. Waiting. There is no one else, he tells her. No one else worth having.

Jennifer's pain had been close to burying her before her desperate act. She resisted for so long. No one knew how hard she worked not to end up here. A desperate woman will do a desperate thing. And then, what if she likes it?

Jennifer knows her marriage looks perfect. James loves that. It's a picture he holds up. And never touches. He hardly lets her touch him. A woman, like all living things, needs *nurture*: both to give and receive. How perfect that she found a gardener. Jennifer's head begins to spin.

"You okay?" he asks.

"Mmm," Jennifer half answers.

"Relax your mind." Andrew kisses her cheek. He must have felt her body tense. "If you were my woman, I would hold you and make love to you. Hold you some more, get a little something to eat with you, make a little more love . . ." He tightens his grip.

"Yeah . . ." Again, Jennifer can hardly hear herself. Hardly knows herself. Tears erupt suddenly. Her need for love, peace of mind, and what she doesn't have, fill her. Will there ever be room for her? She's been so alone and terribly lonely. Jennifer is buried somewhere beneath it all. And now someone has touched her. Has opened her . . .

She can't go back. Can't move forward. What does a way of life look like that she cannot see? Would James be okay without her? Would Andrew appear different in the light of real daily life? Would she have been the greatest fool of all?

"I—" Jennifer can barely speak. "I need to go."

"Hey. Don't leave like this." Andrew pulls her close. "You get so twisted up in your mind. Let me run you a warm bath. You're shaking." Her voice is gone.

Layers of calm envelop Jennifer as she eases into the warm water. She breathes, slowly coming back together. "Thank you," she offers.

Andrew. Fully dressed. Watching her.

"I feel so vulnerable," Jennifer says softly.

"I know."

"I wish our culture had lovers," she says, reaching. "Maybe if we were in Europe, it wouldn't be so hard."

"Maybe this also brings up all the questions you don't want to answer. If you didn't have to be secretive with me, I'd be able to support you through all this."

Jennifer knows he means the sex, which has pushed her to her very edge. Such mystery and grace. And in moments, something almost sinister.

"I'm scared of you."

"You should be."

"I think you're crazy."

"I am, but not in my life. Just here with you. I'm not a typical man. I'm sure I bring up a lot that frightens you."

He has no idea what that means for a woman like her. She lives an ordinary life. She does normal things in a normal world. Jennifer's stomach grumbles.

"I'm starving." She is unable, unwilling, to step out of this dark dance. She feels different when she's with him. He devours her. Why can't she see him clearly? It's as if something in him shifts ever so slightly, so her view of him is always slightly peripheral.

"Me too. I made beans last night." He kisses her forehead. "I'll heat them up."

Jennifer washes her body. Slowly. Feeling the memory of the last few hours. Andrew pleases her in so many ways. And she loves the pleasure she brings him. She can tell he is often surprised by it.

The beans are warm. Spicy. Comforting. How can there simultaneously be such strong connection and dissonance? Moments like this are rare. It's the normal things of life they don't share much of. Eating. Talking. Socializing. Not that at all.

"I need to go." Jennifer stands.

"Come here." Andrew wraps her in a towel.

"Thanks for feeding me. I'm much better."

"I could make you feel even better."

He pulls her in, kissing her. How is it possible? She has been with him, come undone, crawled back to her center . . .

and is willing so soon to jump again into the abyss? Andrew's hands firmly hold her wrists. He walks her backward. Her back presses against the wall. He kisses her neck.

"Jennifer," he whispers close. She dissolves into him. The cycle. Nothing in her can stop this. There are times Jennifer worries she might die from pleasure with this man. Then she worries she will die without it. In between, she just worries.

He moves in every crevice of her. His hands, his mouth, loving every inch. She trembles. Cups his face. His neck. Arms. He pulls her to the floor. Eyes locked. As he moves his body over hers, Jennifer loses all thought. Her life falls away.

"I love you," she gasps.

Andrew's smile spreads. Creeps over his entire being.

"You know I love you, Jennifer."

Kate

Sitting on the outside patio full of mismatched chairs and funky painted tables, the weather is perfect. Despite the sunshine, Kate can't shake her mental fog. Legs crossed, and arms wrapped around herself, she leans toward Nia.

"Why am I so confused?" she asks. Nia listens, holding her coffee mug in both hands. Kate admires her soft beauty. Her deep, thoughtful eyes, strong yet delicate features, and simple, sophisticated sundress.

The sudden pang again.

"Are you all right?" Nia leans forward.

"Just my stomach."

"Are you sick?"

"No, not like that."

Kate can't find the words to even begin to describe what it's like as she's beginning to feel the depth of her emotions.

"What about getting a massage? Kate, I'm looking at you and you're all twisted up. I wish you could see my massage therapist. He's excellent, and he's right around the corner from me. I wish you could come."

Nia lives in their hometown. She had earned her doctorate from the University of Chicago and is now an associate professor of African American studies at Northwestern. Kate wonders what might have happened if she'd at least gotten her master's.

"I've been thinking . . ." Kate's voice trails off.

"About what?"

"What it would be like. To move."

"Move where?"

"I don't know. I miss how I used to feel."

Nia listens intently, then asks, "What do you mean?"

"I'm worried about Ben and Peter. They're growing up Southern California boys. And I miss the Midwest."

"I can understand that. The culture here is very different."

Bringing the mug to her lips, Kate sips slowly, subtly running her tongue along the edge. Hot and earthy. Kate holds her cup close.

"I . . . I used to feel different."

"How so?"

"I felt much more grounded in Evanston. And there's something I can't get past here." She looks down and shakes her head. "It's hard to explain."

"Well, you've got something there. Listen to that. Trust yourself." Nia points to Kate's stomach. "It sounds like your body is saying something. We hold feelings in parts of our bodies. Seriously, it's true."

Kate leans back and closes her eyes, feeling warmth on her face.

"If I moved, I'd sure miss this weather."

"Yes, you would. It's a trade-off." Nia leans back and sips her coffee. "You should see how many coffee shops are in Evanston now. The downtown is really changing."

She hasn't been there in years.

"I'm seeing things in Peter I wonder about. He's growing up in ways I don't get. So much is different here. With other kids and families. Feels like a lack of boundaries."

"That's worth considering."

"Yeah," Kate agrees. "But what would it be like to actually live in Evanston? I mean, I remember. I just wish I knew what it would be like now. And for Peter and Ben. It's hard to imagine. My mom moved away, and I think the fellowship is different, way smaller, but still . . ."

"You wouldn't need to live in South Evanston. You could live near me, closer to the lake and Northwestern. If you're serious about it, bring it up with David. I love the idea, of course. We used to talk about that, remember? It's a big move, though."

"Sounds daunting. And exciting. To start somewhere fresh . . . Nia, it would be so fun to be in Evanston with you."

"So fun." Nia smiles and takes a last sip. "I need more coffee. Do you want some?"

"Please."

As Nia takes the mugs inside, Kate takes in the patio. Her favorite coffee shop, with its eclectic mix of tables and chairs. She thought they would live in Ojai forever. But it's starting to feel restricting.

She had loved growing up in South Evanston, and although she lived in a religious community—shared households, everyone giving their money to the church, no one owning anything, not even a car—the children went to public school. They were known as "the fellowship kids."

As a teenager, going to a huge high school felt freeing. Evanston only had one. There were over one thousand students in her graduating class. And it was incredibly diverse: racially, religiously, economically . . . It didn't matter that Kate didn't have money. Although Evanston was known for its affluent North Shore, many people had much less. She felt no pressure to belong to a clique and had floated from group to group, doing her own thing even after she started doing theater. Kate can't help smiling, imagining Peter and Ben at Evanston Township High School.

Suddenly, Nia is handing her a full, hot mug. They sit silently for a moment.

"I was just thinking about ETHS." Kate laughs. "We had some fun, didn't we?"

"We sure did. We worked hard too."

"You worked harder than I did."

"Maybe a bit."

"Ha! A bit. Miss Valedictorian. I still remember your speech."

"Me too. And I remember you in *Cyrano de Bergerac*." Kate's first big part. She had cried hard when the show closed. Seems like a lifetime ago.

"Does David still work from home?"

"Yep. I don't mind too much. It's convenient. But then there are days, I don't know why—like today, I woke up, and all I wanted was to get out of there."

"That's understandable," Nia gently offers.

What does her life consist of, anyway? She can hardly focus. Since the bus. Since the night she wrote it down—and kept writing. It's as if she is carrying a secret, creating a separate world.

"You're daydreaming." Nia laughs. "Are you seriously considering moving? David has lived in Southern California for a long time."

"I know. But this feels strong. I'm not sure why, exactly."

"Then pick a good time to bring it up." Nia takes a sip. "I think it would be great."

"Maybe"—Kate pauses—"I'll just come without him."

"Who? David?"

"Yeah. Just me and the boys."

Nia looks directly at her. "What is going on, Kate?"

"I don't know." She shrugs. "Just . . ." What to say? She's been holding everything so tight for so long. "Thinking about things. From years ago."

"Like what?"

"Well . . . there was a night . . . back when we lived in LA."

"When was that?" asks Nia.

"I was pregnant with Peter. David went to his office. Said there was something he had to get. He told me he might stop by some bar on the way back for a drink, but probably not because he felt sick." Kate stops and sips her coffee. "It's probably nothing. It's stupid to even bring it up."

"No, it's not." Nia's look urges her on.

"At three in the morning, David still wasn't home. This was before we had cell phones. I called his office, the bar, then two hospitals. Nothing. I even called his sister and her husband. I was panicked. They drove all the way to our house and were just getting out of the car when David walked up. Drunk. He said a guy he knew was bartending and invited some people back to his place for more wine. Said he hadn't called because he knew I'd be sleeping. It was after four in the morning."

Nia raises her eyebrows. "What do you think?"

"I don't know."

"Do you think he was with a woman?"

"I'll never know." Kate shakes her head. "He'd never tell me." The air feels thick.

"That story doesn't add up." Nia shakes her head now.

"I know. David's just . . . checked out. Has been ever since we got married. He wasn't like this at first, when we were dating. In fact, I fell for him because he was so present."

"I remember."

Kate looks up. The sky is bright blue. If only she could disappear into it. "And also—" Her voice breaks.

"This is important." Nia lays her hand on Kate's. "You've been really sad. For a long time."

"I have?" It was noticeable?

Nia nods.

"I—" Kate tries to swallow. She takes another sip of her coffee. "I keep thinking about this time we went to visit his brother. We had to take one of those trams between flights. The airport was huge. I told David clearly—so clearly—to hold Peter's hand tight. Mine were full with Ben, who was a tiny baby, and bags. David promised he would."

"And?"

"The tram was crowded. When the doors opened, we got off. We were walking away, and a voice in my head screamed,

'Turn around *now*!' I did. And you know what? The doors were closing—with Peter inside."

"Oh, Kate."

"Without thinking, my body was moving. Somehow my arm reached through the doors, just in time. I grabbed Peter and pulled him out. I don't know how. It all happened in a flash. And also slow motion."

The bus. Why had she not seen the similarities until this moment? No thought. No fear. No time. Moving with what was happening . . .

"When I asked David what happened," Kate continues, "he said he'd told Peter to hold on to the strap of his bag. He was only three years old."

"Wow . . ."

"Peter had nightmares for months that we left him on the tram. He cried and cried. I would ask him to remember what happened next, in real life, as the doors were closing. He said, 'You saved me.'"

Nia reaches into her pocket. She holds out a small stone. "Here. For you, Kate." Nia places the translucent, white oval in the palm of Kate's hand.

"It's beautiful."

"It's a moonstone. I've thought of it as my 'touchstone.' It was given to me ten years ago, and I was told I would know when to pass it on."

"Nia." Kate smiles through her tears. "Thank you." The stone is smooth and perfect.

"It belongs to you now."

"I love it."

"This is your *life*, Kate," Nia says. "Don't sit back and let it happen."

Suddenly, Kate can't sit any longer. "Hey, let's go for a walk. I need to move."

"That sounds good," Nia agrees.

Touching shoulders as they take their empty mugs to the counter, Kate and Nia share a loving look. She'd told Nia. She'd found the words. And Nia heard her, then had given her a special gift.

Kate continues to notice the trees all day, set beautifully against the bright blue sky. She imagines herself soaring. Her thoughts take her to David's childhood. His wounds were part of what drew her to him; she knows that now. Will she ever overcome them? And what of her own?

)))

"You're not really here." Gripping the moonstone. It's hard to swallow.

"What do you mean?" David sounds defensive. "I'm right here."

Why does she always bring up conversation with David in bed? "Know how in your house you were checked out? Growing up. How you coped?"

"Yeah." David clearly doesn't want to engage.

"That's what you do." Kate tries to remain calm. "Still."

"What are you talking about?"

"You." She breathes into her stomach, tight with nerves. "What it's like living with you."

"Where's this coming from?"

"It just is."

"Why? Why now?"

"I don't know. I'm just . . . so . . . confused."

"Okay." David is evasive.

"And it's not just now. It's . . . There's a lot. And I don't deal with it. I don't know how to." She looks at David. "I'm not your mother."

"I know you're not!"

"No, you don't! Not really. You walk around like . . . like I don't even know what. I feel like I'm living with a ghost."

"I'm right here!"

"No, David. You're not."

David lets out an odd, pinched sound.

Kate continues. "Maybe you don't know what I'm talking about. But you'd better wake up." Heart racing. "If you don't want to be here—tell me. I'd rather be alone for real than keep doing this."

David stares out the window. Silent.

"I've never felt so alone as since I married you." Something in her is breaking open. "And it's not just now. It's the whole thing. Our entire marriage."

No response. Silence.

Kate throws the covers off and walks straight to the bathroom. She crumbles. Tears come fast and hard. Her insides turn out. She cries for the illusion she's been living. For her children. For the devastating realization—she has married the wrong man. She wants to go home.

Jennifer

"Do you have a boyfriend besides Daddy?" The question is shocking, slipping sweetly from her daughter's mouth.

"What do you think?" asks Jennifer.

"I think you do," Chloe says, her tone matter-of-fact.

"Do you think Daddy has a girlfriend besides me?"

"I don't know." Jennifer is used to innocent, unnerving conversations. Chloe has always been intuitive, if not psychic, but hardly ever aware, and never emotional about her uncanny statements.

Jennifer is amused and a little relieved at the frankness of this exchange—even as her heart races. She won't lie to her daughter. She feels somewhere in Chloe's soul, she knows. She would never purposefully dismiss her daughter's instincts. Jennifer has become good at responding to her children's questions with questions of her own.

The rest of the day seems to exist within a waking-dream state. How can she hold together the very thing she is undoing? At what point will she find herself too close to the edge? What if she falls? Jennifer is only willing to risk so much.

Her children. She is grateful for this bond, how it has the strength to ground her. There are times she feels the hot danger of not having her own clear boundaries.

)))

"Jennifer?" James. Home. In the kitchen.

"Oh! You scared me," Jennifer lets out a nervous giggle.

"Sorry I'm so late. Are the kids in bed?" James puts down his briefcase. He looks handsome even at the end of a long day.

"Yeah, a half hour ago. Hungry?"

"No. I had a late lunch meeting," says James. "Remember?"

"Yeah. Oh yeah."

"I ate way too much." He stares at her. "You okay?"

Jennifer's eyes slowly meet his. Then, without warning, hands immersed in dishwater, the tethers holding her life together begin to fray. She feels something in her throat, moving up. Is this happening? She isn't ready. She didn't plan it.

She chokes, letting out a cough.

"What's wrong? Are you sick?"

Jennifer shakes her head. It's happening. James is motionless. "What is it?"

She moves almost completely out of herself. Watching from somewhere above her body. Distanced from the unthinkable.

"I'm . . . having . . . an affair." If it weren't for the warmth of the water on her hands, Jennifer feels she would collapse.

Her disbelief at her own words is as great to her as to her husband. James slowly forms his first question. His voice searing.

"How long?"

"A year." James sits. She sees he does not know her. She doesn't know herself.

"Who is it?"

"Andrew."

"Andrew?"

"Yeah." His disbelief is heavy. Smothering. Jennifer feels she is sinking. There is no ground. No one to help her.

"Why did you have to tell me? Why couldn't you just stop?" James implores. "You shouldn't have told me."

Her stomach implodes. Why had she?

"I never thought you were capable of this."

No one did. Not even her. Time turns to metaphor. Jennifer's brain shuts down. Survival. The questions come. She answers. James's words. Disconnected. She responds. Automatically. Her secret is out. Now she knows—this is how it happens. Just like this. On an ordinary evening, for no reason at all, a woman breaks. Breaks everything. Shakes the whole world.

The evening begins its long descent. Darkness envelops as James holds Jennifer hostage to her sins. She is Eve. She has willingly eaten the apple. She still has the taste of it in her mouth. His questions are endless. His words, ruthless.

"Where did you meet him? Did he go down on you? He's so old—so ugly! What if you'd gotten pregnant! How could you do this to our family? Cheating bitch!"

Hers is now a world of misdeeds. Unforgivable shame. This is what she must bear. Not only for her wrongdoing. For telling the truth. Those had been his first words, hadn't they? *Why did you have to tell me? You shouldn't have told me!* Why would he say such a thing?

Jennifer is unable to ask. She cannot even hold the question. Her ears hurt from hearing, over and over, how horrible she is. Her eyes burn from crying. Her mouth is dry. Stomach empty. And her heart—shattered.

James—with his judgment, condemnation, and hate—takes Jennifer apart slowly, deliberately, methodically.

By the time dawn reveals another day, Jennifer exists only as a fragment of herself. She finally lies down. Begging for mercy.

"Please." Able to endure no more. "I can't—" Cradled in her bed.

A mistake. Jennifer has made a terrible, irrevocable mistake. Wrapped in her husband's righteous wrath, she lies broken. Hope gone. Love gone. She slips into raw, restless sleep for a single hour before it is time to wake the children, help them get ready, and take them to school.

)))

THE DAYS THAT FOLLOW JENNIFER'S CONFESSION BLUR. Disoriented moments stretch into elongated hours. She deserves any punishment James inflicts. She has fallen. She weeps at her deception. Overwhelming regret. She feels for her husband's innocence and his love for her and the children.

"How could you do this?" His voice echoes through her. "How could you threaten the family? How could you sleep with two people at the same time?"

From the moment she rises until deep into the night, Jennifer accepts his rage. Absorbs it. She is worthless. Desperate.

Most of all, she is frightened. She has seen her husband's anger before, when directed at his business associates, but never has she been its target. And never has he felt so betrayed.

The week is endless. Sleepless. Terror filled.

Jennifer takes the children to school and picks them up. She volunteers in their classrooms and brings their friends over to play. And in between these activities that hold sunlight and people and the routines of the day, Jennifer sinks into quiet despair.

There is a hell that happens in her home when the sun goes down. No one sees it. No one knows.

Then . . . finally . . . for reasons beyond her knowing, one day something in Jennifer shifts. She has had enough. Her acceptance of James's cruel dominance is over. She reaches deep within—moving through her silence, past her passivity—and begins to feel herself. Finally able to speak, Jennifer turns to face her husband.

"I'm done." Her voice is clear.

"With what?"

"This. Your words. Your torment."

"You think I'm your tormentor?" He is incredulous.

Jennifer stares at James. She watches anger flash across his face. Rage. And in that moment, she sees something else. Unrecognizable.

He opens his mouth. His throat catches. He tries again. Something is in the way, blocking his words. They are unable to reach his tongue.

Jennifer has never, in all the years she's known him, witnessed such a thing. James is a master of words. He is known for it. He can talk his way through anything.

He tries a third time. And as his breath moves out, a guttural sound escapes his lips. It is thick. Wordless. He appears to be at a complete loss. Then she sees it . . . fear.

"I wanted to tell you," he says, "for so long . . ." Jennifer stays completely still. "There was someone else . . . the first three years."

Her heart beats in her ears. The ground begins to move. This can't be happening.

Jennifer shakes her head. Surreal. The first three years? But they'd been in love. Gotten married. Chloe . . . Jimmy . . . Now it is she who asks her first question.

"Who?"

"Charlotte."

That name. She had known of Charlotte, a woman in Northern California. A friend of a friend of James's.

Then, everything begins to connect. He was with Charlotte during the first three years of their marriage. During her pregnancy with Chloe. Nursing. Jennifer's heart plummets. Such an innocent, magical time . . .

Yes, that was when everything had changed. He was no longer there for her, sweet to her. Just months after their wedding, he was a different person. She thinks of his trips . . . his literal and figurative absences. He had become so unkind. Uncaring. Jennifer remembers his confusing comments and constant criticism of her. His withholding. She didn't measure up. She never knew why. Now she does.

"I am so sorry." James's face looks relieved.

"Were there more?" she asks. He looks at the floor. There is a long pause. "How many?"

"It won't help you to know."

Jennifer sinks further. "When did it start?"

"When we were dating." Even then. Before they'd married. Before he had tricked and trapped her. "But never here. Never with anyone in town." His pride is unmistakable.

"How many?" Jennifer asks again.

"I'm not sure." James avoids her eyes.

"Tell me."

"Maybe . . . I don't know. Eight? Ten?"

Jennifer feels a complete remove. James's words breeze through her. He is a stranger. She never would have married this man. A numbness overcomes her.

Jennifer walks to the kitchen counter and picks up her purse and car keys. She is only movement now. "Thank you. It all makes sense." As she reaches for the doorknob, she looks at James. "I'll be back in the morning. Early." She opens the door. "For the children." And closes it.

YEAR TWO

MOVING

Kate

She can hardly believe it. North Evanston is everything Kate hoped it would be. Magnificent trees, beautiful homes, and a lively downtown. Lake Michigan, with its walking and biking paths, beaches, and large rocks lining the shore. She loved climbing on those rocks when she was little.

"How long were we in our Ojai house? Five years?"

"I'm not sure." Nia takes a sip of her wine. "Kate, I'm so glad you're back, here and now. Able to walk downtown, along the lake."

"Remember how big those rocks were?"

"They were gigantic! How much fun did we have, hopping from one to the next? I loved to see how fast I could go. I twisted my ankle that one time, remember?"

"I was so jealous of your crutches!"

"Oh yeah. It was fun to have crutches the first few days. Then I just wanted to play during recess." Nia smiles at Kate.

"You stayed with me, though. Playing jacks . . . making up stories with the bugs."

"Wow, Nia, I forgot that."

"We loved it, and they were good stories too. Our imaginations were really something."

"Remember the clouds?" They would get lost in them for hours. "How we'd see shapes."

"And animals . . . faces, even. Lying in the grass, just watching the clouds."

"And my favorite: lying on the warm sand, and then running into the water." Kate smiles. "I know I'm supposed to love the ocean, but there's something about Lake Michigan. The only spanking I ever got was because I wouldn't come out. I couldn't." Her mom was furious. But her dad gave the punishment. "I can't explain—I couldn't stop swimming. I swear I could breathe underwater. My lips were completely blue."

"You were a fish in that water. Hey, how about this . . ." Nia lights up. "Do you remember the tornado slide? How much fun was that? Talk about huge! It's completely wild because it was a good slide, no doubt, but back then it was downright magical."

"It totally was!"

"And the merry-go-round, we absolutely traveled on that. Remember how we'd hold on and lean out . . . then say one, two, three, *in*!" Nia leans in. "And we'd all pull in at the same time! We spun so fast . . . for so long. How do kids do that?"

Kate laughs, bringing her wine to her lips.

"Too bad none of that is there anymore," Nia reflects. "The swings are, though. We would see how high we could go before leaping off!"

"We were nuts!"

They laugh and shake their heads.

"But your favorite was the beach." Nia plays with the stem of her glass. "I'm glad you can have that with Peter and Ben now."

Kate nods. "Me too."

"Making sandcastles. All those worlds we created. And sand angels."

"Sand angels!" Kate squeals, remembering looking up at the sky while flying on the ground. "Like snow angels."

"And endlessly drawing and coloring butterflies." Nia is nodding. "And look at you, Kate. You got packed up. You packed everything up . . . and you moved your whole family here. I'm so proud of you."

"Thank you, Nia. It took a lot. And was so worth it."

"Evanston is better with you in it, that's for sure." Nia pauses for a moment. "And how's David?"

"It's funny. He went to college here . . . I grew up here . . . It just feels right. He's doing okay."

"Yeah? Well, that's good to hear . . ." Nia looks up as the waiter sets two plates on the table.

"That looks incredible." Kate's mouth waters.

"You've been going nonstop. I have too. Tonight, we relax and enjoy."

The waiter empties the bottle into their glasses, asking, "Is there anything else I can bring you ladies? More wine?"

"None for me," says Nia. "Thank you."

"I'm fine too."

"Let me know if there's anything you need."

As the waiter leaves, Kate takes a bite of her food.

"Wow, this pasta..." Kate lets out a dramatic moan, then continues. "You know, David has breakfast with his two best friends from college every Monday morning."

"That is perfect."

"Yeah, he needed that. He really didn't want to come at first... and he's good now. In certain ways, at least."

"He has old connections here, genuine friendships. There's nothing like friends from back in the day, as we well know."

"As we well do."

What a luxury to have a night out. Kate really has been going nonstop getting everything together. For everyone.

"How are Peter and Ben adjusting?"

"Oh, Peter. Sweet boy." Kate's heart hurts thinking about it. "He ate lunch alone the first two weeks at school."

"Poor little guy."

"I know. I was a wreck. All I wanted was to take him out of there. Or pay some kid to sit with him. He's making friends now, thank goodness."

"I'm so glad." Nia smiles. "And how about Ben?"

"He did a one-eighty! He didn't like school in California. Here he waved good-bye the first day and never looked back. Under the category of 'you never know.'"

"That is really something."

"I know."

"It all sounds good, Kate... seriously."

How long had she and Nia talked of living in the same place one day? Since grade school?

"And what's the name of your therapist? Marla?"

"Marta."

"Right . . . Marta. So, what is she like?"

"There's something about her . . ." Kate has never known a woman like her. "She's in her early sixties, I think, and . . . unusual. Intuitive. Tall and thin—but strong. She has a slight accent, something European. I see her again tomorrow."

"How often do you go?"

"We're pretty much looking at once a week right now. I really like her. I trust her."

"Kate, that's great. Really," says Nia. "It makes so much possible."

"Do we want more wine? Maybe a glass?"

"Oh, I'm still good with this, but go ahead."

Kate leans over, pointing to her glass. "Sir? Can I have one more, please?"

She turns back to Nia. "What about you? Seeing anyone?"

"Oh . . . well . . ." Nia sighs. "It's not easy . . . with working so much. I'm fine. I mean, I'd like to be in a relationship, a good one. A serious one. But I'm not looking to just fill my time. He would have to be . . . you know what I'm trying to say. It would have to be special."

Special. Yes . . .

Nia continues, "If it's meant to be, it will happen. I'm keeping my eyes open, so there's that. The last date I had was right before you moved here. So, we'll see . . ."

"It'll happen."

"I hope so." Nia smiles. "It would be nice to have someone to come home to . . . and to have him come home to me." Nia looks so tender. Kate suddenly feels self-conscious.

"I'm sorry I've been talking so much about myself."

"Oh, Kate, it's . . ." Nia slowly exhales. "I'm just happy to be out with you. I was looking forward to this. I'm also glad things have settled down at work a bit. They were pretty crazy there for a while. We've made a few changes, and it feels a lot better."

Why is it so easy to think Nia has it all figured out?

"I do wonder sometimes . . . ," Nia muses, "if we really can have it all." She looks like her little-girl self for a moment.

"Me too."

The waiter places a glass of wine on the table in front of Kate. She watches him as he walks away, then smiles at Nia.

"I . . . I've been writing something."

"Well, you're full of surprises. What is it?"

"I'm not sure yet." Kate laughs, feeling suddenly shy about it, even with Nia. "I never know what's going to come out until I've written it. But it's very intense. The lead character is a woman. And I don't know . . ."

"Oh, I'd love to read it . . . if you'd want, at some point." Nia pauses. "But I can tell by your face that's not going to happen."

"No, no, not yet. Not even close. I was worried even to tell you. Or anyone"

"Kate . . . why?"

"I just . . ." Nia is so accomplished. "I don't know. I feel embarrassed. I don't have any sort of background in writing. Or English. Or anything."

"You know more than you think you do. You were a theater major. I'll bet you anything you've soaked up more about story and character development than you realize. And think about it . . . dialogue."

"Huh." Kate hadn't really thought about it.

"Don't worry about any of that," Nia reassures her. "Just keep writing. Keep doing what you're doing."

What is the cost of doing her creative work? What's the cost of not doing it? And how can she continue without taking too much from her family?

"I worry about the boys. When I write . . . I go somewhere else."

"They know how much you love them. It's healthy for Ben and Peter to see their mother doing things. So what if you're not perfect in every moment," Nia adds gently.

"I know. I'm just . . . I get scared."

"You moved your family—David, of all people—across the country based on your gut. You don't have anything to be afraid of. And you're writing!" Nia's eyes look almost golden. Kate spent all of third grade wishing she looked just like her. "And if you ever forget, or get seriously worried, or whatever . . . call me."

"I will." Kate nods. "And you too."

"It really is good you moved back, Kate . . . in a number of ways."

"I'm so glad I came home."

☽ ☽ ☽

Glad to be back in Marta's office, Kate looks around. It's sparse, yet comfortable. Something in her is beginning to relax.

"I thought things would be a lot different with David—" Kate stares at the carpet. "I had dinner with my friend Nia, the one I told you about, and realized how good it is to be back. I just . . . I don't know about my marriage. I wonder if I might rather be alone."

Marta's face softens, her eyes intent on Kate. "Where do you feel it in your body?"

"My body?" Kate thinks a moment. Her eyes rest on the large painting leaning against the wall. The painted plant blends effortlessly into the dark soil it rests in. Why hasn't Marta hung it up? "The middle of my stomach, definitely my stomach. And my heart. Sometimes my throat." She suddenly feels like crying.

"Take care of your nervous system and the rest will fall into place. Someone told me that years ago. And I've found it to be mostly true." Marta pauses. "Kate, are you exercising?"

"No."

"Eating well? Getting enough sleep?" Kate has no idea what she's been eating.

"No. And probably not." Kate realizes she's been taking care of everyone else through this transition and has completely neglected herself. Then she sees something else. "It's not just the move. This is what I do. I care for my boys. David. Everyone. Everyone but me." She looks at Marta and surprises herself. "I've had it!"

"Good!"

The blue walls. How can a therapist's office be so comforting? Something beneath her confusion is beginning to emerge. Anger.

"I'm going to get a massage. Nia's been saying it would help me, and she has a great massage therapist. And I'll start walking again." Why hasn't she made time for that? "I love walking." Kate suddenly sees that when she looks at the possibility of divorcing David, she glimpses not only having space from him and her hurt—but also a way to take a break. She curls her legs beneath her, wanting to lay her head on the sturdy arm of the couch. "What about me and David?"

"See if you can find space for yourself within the marriage," Marta answers. "Once you begin to do that, we will look at the marriage itself."

"Promise?"

"Yes. And also, remember to breathe. It's so easy for us to forget the most basic and important things when we need them the most."

Kate takes in a deep breath and releases it.

"One more thing before we end today. I want to check in with you about the religious commune here you said you grew up in." Marta tilts her head slightly. "How does that feel to you now that you're back in Evanston?"

"Oh." Kate hasn't thought much about it. "Honestly, I don't think it's an issue, not really. We live in a totally different area, and that feels like a long time ago. I'm so busy with everything."

"Well, know that if it does come up for you, we can talk about it."

After her appointment, Kate eats a turkey sandwich and a large bowl of tomato soup. Then she collapses, sleeping for two and a half hours.

)))

Suddenly awake, Kate remembers she was dreaming she stood alone at the top of a children's play structure. There were several slides, steps, and ladders. She was paralyzed with fear, not knowing which way to go. Then, taking a deep breath, she chose a slide and slid smoothly to the bottom. As she got up and walked around the corner, Kate came face-to-face with a real live lion. He was enormous. She felt terrified. Then she became aware of a single flower in her hand and held it out to him. An offering. The lion accepted her gift and talked with her for a long time.

Jennifer

JENNIFER'S MOUTH IS DRY. SHE CAN HARDLY SWALLOW. SHE stares at the beige wall. A crack runs from the middle near the window all the way to the ceiling. Looks like there's been water damage. Can cracks, if they run too deep, ever be repaired?

"Jennifer?" She looks at Lark.

Jennifer marvels at her therapist's elegance. Her clothes are simple and flattering, her hair perfectly cut to frame her classic face. Jennifer hopes she will age as gracefully. She wonders what Lark looked like when she was younger. Most of all, Jennifer admires Lark's ability to move easily between emotion and intellect.

"Is there anything you want to say to James?"

Jennifer looks at her husband. She's seen him only in brief, dutiful encounters. James has Chloe and Jimmy two days a week.

"I don't know." She wants to be home in her new neighborhood. In her little apartment with natural light, exposed brick, and a welcoming flower-lined courtyard. Home eating pancakes with her children while they watch cartoons. "I'm not even mad," Jennifer continues, "I just don't care anymore."

"And how about you, James?" Lark asks. "Do you feel it is over in your marriage?"

"No . . . ," he mumbles. "I . . . don't want it to be over."

Jennifer can hardly keep from rolling her eyes. "It's been months, and I'm happier than I've been since I married you."

"What about the kids?" James shoots back.

"What *about* the kids?" Jennifer counters. "And what about *me*? You have no idea how you even feel. It's 'the kids' and 'I'm breaking up the family.' Your sweeping statements."

"But I think—" James tries.

"I am so sick of hearing everything from your cerebral little world," Jennifer interrupts. "Everything that happens in your head is *only* in your head. It's not here. Nobody experiences it." Silence. "I think you're a coward," she dares.

Again, silence.

"I . . . am a coward," James agrees.

"Well," Lark offers, "if you are done, then you are done. There's no point working on this if one of you doesn't want to. But you will always have a relationship through the children. They are still very young."

Jennifer's heart lurches. "I wouldn't even be in this room if it weren't for them."

Is James crying?

"Do you think you need more time?" Lark asks. "Do you want to continue to live separately and come here once in a while? Or every week? What do you think?"

Jennifer tries to think. She wants to walk away. To take back the years James stole from her. Claim her children as her own. He should move on, turn some twenty-year-old into his prey. That's how he likes them. Young, naive, and vulnerable. "I can't go back," she says.

There is no doubt. James is crying. He cries for a long time, his face still buried in his hands. Lark places a box of tissues on the table. Nobody says anything. Jennifer checks her watch. The room feels suddenly stuffy. Nausea overwhelms her.

"James," Lark suggests, "would you like to talk with me alone?"

He nods, hands still hiding his sorrow. Jennifer catches herself momentarily feeling his pain.

"I'll go."

"Why don't we meet again next week. Give you both a bit of time . . ."

Jennifer picks up her sweater and purse.

"Call me if you need to." Lark's concern, so genuine. "Anytime."

The door closes heavily behind her. Dizzy. Mouth dry. Jennifer walks quickly down the stairs. A Coke from the little Thai place next door. What a relief she doesn't have to sit next to James on the drive home. They had tried it once, two weeks earlier. She couldn't bear having him so near, in such a small, enclosed space. Was this the third time they'd seen Lark? The third since it all happened. Since the crack became so deep their entire lives had fallen into it.

Jennifer finds her keys and climbs into her car. The Coke is cold and sweet. It's good she got it. Her mind is spent. Her eyes want to close. As she pulls out of her parking space, she glances up at the second-floor window. James is in there. James may still be crying.

How different he was when they met. Handsome and kind. Now Jennifer sees him as an expert manipulator, creating trancelike states with his words. He did this to women he wanted to sleep with. There had been many before her, she always knew that. How had she thought it would stop with her? She thought he had done everything he wanted. Her naiveté feels humiliating. The drive is long, and the Coke helps. She feels heavy. Layered with sadness and spite.

Jennifer pulls directly into the preschool parking lot. Jimmy comes running. "Mama!" He throws his arms around her, his hug restoring her.

"Hi, sweet boy! I'm so happy to see you."

"Me too."

Jennifer showers him with kisses as she buckles him into his car seat and hands him a juice box. She plans ahead now and has a twelve-pack of apple juice in her car.

"We going home?"

"Yes, sweetie, remember? To Mama's home?"

"Oh." Jimmy looks confused.

"Is that okay?"

"Okay. My yellow truck is there."

"Yes. And your red one is at Daddy's."

"When do I go there?" he asks.

"In two days."

Jimmy in the rearview mirror. Drinking through his straw while rubbing his right ear. Such a comforting habit. He'd done that since he was a baby nursing. Jennifer would have no more children. She'd always thought of having another. Not definitely, but possibly. No third child. No husband . . .

A lover . . . Is this what she wants? She doesn't want her children to know. She's ambivalent about his visits, still sneaking him in on random nights. She doesn't want his calls. Only sex. Andrew is still, by her own doing, separate from her life. It's painful for him, Jennifer can tell. He doesn't understand. She wants only to feel his body. His warmth. She's drawn to him in darkness. Andrew pushes her boundaries. It's good somehow, to have that removed from her real life. Away from her children. When she is with him, Jennifer moves into parts of herself she never knew existed. She touches something lost. A frightening ecstasy.

What if she replaced her husband with a lover who also changed when things became real? She has never been like this before. So protected. If anything, she was open to a fault. Now, Jennifer feels herself creating walls and boundaries.

She checks Jimmy in the rearview mirror. Sound asleep, juice box still in hand. She'll drive around for a while, then go pick up Chloe. So much of her time is spent getting from place to place. At least now she can breathe. Jennifer can create her own home. She rarely has the television on. She couldn't stand that about James, his addiction to the screen. Jennifer feels more in control of the environment she creates for her children. Still, they are with him sometimes. Without her. What is that like for them?

Lark is right. They are still very young.

Why does freedom have to come at such a cost? Jennifer has seen couples divorce and later regret it, especially the effects on the children. She also knows of a woman who left her husband only to end up with another man who seemed different—but in time turned out not to be. She might as well stay with James. At least he is the children's father. And a good provider.

But Jennifer has also seen couples break up and grow personally, eventually finding more appropriate mates. She knows of one woman who left an unhealthy marriage and met a man who loved her in all the ways she'd always dreamed of. They had a baby together, and her children from her first marriage grew to accept the situation, and even thrive. They were connected to their new stepfather not only through their mother's happiness but also through their new little sister.

What is Jennifer's fate? And why is she even for a moment thinking of working things out with James? If her mothering were a lesser part of her, she knows she would've already filed for divorce. But she will not be any version of her own mother. Whatever the outcome, working with Lark will help. It will provide a process and support for them as they deal with what has happened. And what will happen next.

Jennifer sighs heavily, aware she is both betrayed and betrayer. Because she holds each position, she cannot claim one and judge the other. She is the same as her husband. He is the same as she is. Yet the way it all happened, the timeline and specifics, sets them apart. Jennifer has changed. She knows she has. For the better. But she is also surviving, helping her children, dealing with day-to-day life. She knows the work with Lark is important, but so far, she has only been able to feel herself at a distance in that room. She isn't ready to share her ambivalence, fear, and confusion. She may never be.

Immediately after James's final confession, she moved out and voiced only her intent to divorce. Jennifer met with a lawyer.

He was nice and extremely helpful. None of the drama would influence custody or alimony. They live in a no-fault state. But she might lose more time with her children. Many divorced couples are given a fifty-fifty split. She couldn't bear that. Jennifer told the lawyer she needed some time and would call him soon.

When she pulls up to the school, Chloe runs out.

"Hey, sweetie. Jimmy is sleeping. Be as quiet as you can."

Chloe slides into her seat and buckles herself in. "I was scared you weren't coming."

Jennifer feels a pang. There's been an undeniable regression in her daughter. "You want to get an ice cream?"

"No. I just want to go home."

What does *home* mean to Chloe? "Okay. Maybe we can bake cookies. I think I have chocolate chips."

"I'm not hungry." She always used to be hungry. "Can we go by our real house?" she continues. "I want to get something."

Real house. "Sweetheart, we can't. You can get it in two days. When you stay with Daddy."

"But I need it."

"What is it? Is it important?"

"It's . . ." Chloe's voice falters. "Nothing."

Jennifer takes a quick peek. Chloe stares out the window. She feels her daughter's conflict—the need to be held but also to push away. Hot tears sting Jennifer's eyes.

Nothing is working. Jennifer's body feels singed with pain. Somehow, she must keep going. If she doesn't listen to herself now, she never will. She has to continue to move forward. Whatever that means.

Kate

"I want to share something with you." Kate takes a purposeful breath. "I never told anyone. You'll think I'm crazy."

Marta's eyes are inquisitive. "It takes quite a lot for me to think someone's crazy."

Kate believes her. "Okay, this was two years ago. When we lived in Ojai. I was taking a bath, and suddenly, I had in my mind, or heard a voice in my head or something, that I was to be at a certain coffee shop at one o'clock. I was annoyed because that was in twenty minutes." Kate stops and shakes her head. "It's too weird."

"Why are you hesitant to share this?"

"I'm . . ." She's at a loss. "It's just . . . it's honestly . . . unbelievable. It's like something I would dream. But it happened. For real."

"I'd love to hear it." Marta's tone is reassuring. "But if you'd rather take some time, maybe write it down at home . . ."

"No, I want to say it." Kate remembers Marta's advice and takes another breath. "So, I go. I take a book and sit at a table outside. I'm reading and kind of looking up once in a while. There are two people talking at a table near me and a man handing out pieces of paper. He gives me one, something about the spring equinox. This is where it gets weird . . ."

"Uh-huh, go on."

"I suddenly feel overwhelmed. The woman at the table near me is talking so loudly, I can't take it. I get up to leave. I don't even know why I'm there. I turn the corner of the building to go to my car—and almost run right into the man. Literally. The one who handed out the flyers. We just stare at each other."

Marta waits patiently.

"He's looking at me in this way . . . like he's seeing right into me. Then he says, 'May I ask you a question?' I say, 'Yes.' And he says, '*Who are you?*'"

Time and place seem to subtly shift.

"I look at him," Kate continues, "and am completely empty. I answer, 'I don't know.' It felt like . . . it was a different reality."

"And what did he say?" An unusual feeling inhabits the room. The walls in Marta's office almost move. Kate places her hands on either side of her body, feeling the solidity of the couch beneath her.

"He asks if I'll talk with him for a few minutes, and I agree." Kate feels weightless. "He tells me there are certain people on the planet at this time who vibrate at a higher frequency than most. He can see it. Something about people's auras. He says he recognizes me as one of them."

Kate waits for Marta to say something. She doesn't.

"He asks me why I'm so scared. And I answer—as if I'd known him for a long time—that I'm scared of this part of me that doesn't fit in the world. It's different. And I don't know how to be with it—especially with my husband. I tell the man things I didn't even know I was thinking." Kate brushes a tear away. "Then he looks at me really serious."

Marta waits.

"He says, 'It's almost time for you to step up to the plate.'"

Marta looks thoughtful. "That is quite something."

"I'll never forget the exact wording. The way he said it."

"Yes . . ."

"Marta." Kate swallows hard. "Do you think I'm crazy?"

"No," she says softly. "Do you?"

Kate laughs and shakes her head. "I don't know. No. I mean, that really happened." She raises her eyebrows. "And then . . . he asks permission to greet me in his tradition. We touch forehead to forehead. Soul to soul."

"How did that feel?"

"Good. Really good."

"It is something to be truly seen by another." Marta, so wise.

"It was like he was seeing something in me I haven't even glimpsed."

"I think in your dreaming you have. From what you've shared with me."

Kate is nodding, thinking . . . Her dreams have been vivid.

"There is a lot in there, in your dreaming. Do you write them down?"

"I try," Kate says. "The big ones stay with me. For years."

They sit quietly. It feels peaceful.

"That is quite an encounter you had with this man. I wonder," Marta ponders, "if there might be a parallel between the lion dream and this experience. The way you turned a corner—and think about the metaphor in that—he was right there, a large presence, who saw you, and spoke directly to you."

Kate feels both removed and very present. "I never would've thought of that."

"When you called me, you were very affected by that lion."

"I couldn't wait to tell you." She nods. "Oh! I almost forgot something! As we were saying good-bye, the man asked me why I came there. I told him I was taking a bath, and it suddenly came into my head so strongly to be there at exactly one o'clock. He threw his head back and started laughing. He laughed and laughed, still laughing as he walked away."

"Interesting. And why do you think you went? It would have been very easy to stay in your bath."

"I don't know." Kate shrugs. "It was loud in my head. Like I had an appointment."

"A kind of agreement?"

"Yeah. Like if I didn't go, I would've missed something important."

"What interests me most is that you chose to listen and then acted on it." Marta looks focused. "I think there are few people who know how to listen this deeply. And then to actually go . . ."

"I didn't even consider not going."

"But this was a choice on your part. There was risk involved."

"It felt like that."

"Yes. That—and your lion dream . . . bear with me," Marta muses, "I'm just free-associating here, but there are, at times, unusual experiences that bring us out of our ordinary, pretty mundane lives. Like this man speaking to you in the way he did, at the level of soul. It can be very difficult for someone in our society to have a way of understanding this."

"You're about the only person I would tell." Maybe Nia . . .

"Yes, I understand. And I also feel it's possible there's an association, or similarity somehow, with this . . . and the experience you shared with me about the bus."

The bus.

"Do you remember in what order they happened?"

"Huh." Kate tries to think. "Oh, I absolutely do. The bus happened after."

"Bear with me again . . . as this is not coming from a place of logic." Marta is deep in thought. "Is it possible your encounter with this man, particularly what he said about it almost being time for you to step up to the plate, was, somehow, a foreshadowing of sorts . . . about what was to come . . . with the bus?"

This feels mind-blowing. Kate had never connected the two. She certainly did step up with the bus.

"Whoa—"

"Now is a good time to take a deep breath."

Kate does. Pausing within the intensity of certain moments is becoming increasingly important. And so easy to forget. They again sit in silence, until Kate breaks it.

"You know, I had a recurring nightmare when I was little. I've never told anyone. I had no way to understand it."

Marta looks at the clock on the side table. "We have time."

"I was running and running from a man who was chasing me, wearing a mask. I'd wake up absolutely terrified."

"What did the mask look like?"

"I don't know how to describe it, really. I can draw it, though."

Marta tears a piece of paper from a small notepad next to her chair. She hands it to Kate, along with a pen. Kate draws a picture of a simple mask and shows it to Marta.

"Hmm, I wonder something . . ."

Marta gets up and walks over to her bookcase. She pulls a book from the top shelf and opens it. She finds the page she is looking for and hands it to Kate.

"Indigenous healing masks," Kate reads. "Wow. It looked like some of these."

"They can be used by shamans and healers. Feel free to take it with you."

Kate looks from the masks to Marta. "Thank you."

Kate leaves Marta's office, book in hand. What if since childhood she had been running from something that was trying to heal, not hurt, her? What if it was not an attack but an invitation?

During dinner that night, she fights the urge to share all of this with David. Why the impulse to run from him too? Kate wants to break free of something. And it feels like the marriage is what confines her.

Jennifer

"Will you meet me?" Jennifer paces, unable to stay still.

"Sure, Jen. What time?"

"Twelve. At the usual?" She switches the phone to her right ear. "I get Jimmy at two."

"No problem. See you in an hour. And, Jen?"

"Yeah?"

"It's gonna be okay."

Lunch with Betty will be good. Checking the time quickly, Jennifer lies on her bed. Just for a moment. Her body feels tired. Her bedroom is coming along nicely. Maybe she should paint it. And add some inexpensive throw pillows. What an unexpected pleasure, to begin putting her apartment together. Making it her own. The phone rings, startling her.

"Hello?" she answers.

"Can I come over?" Her body quivers at the sound of his voice.

"Where are you?"

"Down the street. I can see your house from here."

"I'm meeting a friend in fifty minutes."

"That's fifty minutes of pleasure."

"Andrew."

"Come on . . ."

"I'm about to shower."

"Leave your door unlocked." Her desire renders her helpless. She hangs up. Why can't she resist him?

The water is warm and reassuring. Jennifer hears the front door, then movement she can't make out. The shower curtain pulls back. Andrew steps in.

"Hey, baby." He smiles.

Andrew wraps his arms around her, heat and comfort pouring over Jennifer. Andrew, ever attentive. It feels so good to be wanted. They wash each other in silence. Taking time. Lingering. He turns off the water, grabs a towel, and dries off her body in what feels like gentle worship. When he is done, he dries himself with the same towel and turns to her.

He holds her face in his hands. "I love you, Jennifer." Andrew's eyes are clear.

Taking her hand, he leads her to the bed. He lies Jennifer on her back and begins touching her skin. First her toes, then traveling slowly up her legs. He moves perfectly along her body, pleasing her as his hands are guided by her curves. He comes at last to her mouth, the source of her deep breathing. He places his lips on hers. Kisses her. Jennifer reaches to feel his longing and guides him to her. As she feels him move within her, she unexpectedly gasps.

"I love you," he says again. His eyes do not leave hers. Jennifer feels the line remove from separate selves . . .

"I love you," she says now.

☽ ☽ ☽

"I am so sorry, Betty." Jennifer rushes in.

"Oh, no problem!"

It's a relief Betty is easygoing. She's all done up, as always. Her blouse matches her big, bright-lipstick smile.

"I ordered the brie appetizer. How about a glass of wine? Looks like you could use it."

"Oh no. That obvious?"

Jennifer feels her cheeks. Hot. Probably bright pink.

"Only to me, Jen." Betty winks. "Don't worry. I'm sure it was well worth being ten minutes late. Hey, I'm jealous!"

"Don't be." Jennifer means it. Appetizers arrive, along with two glasses of white wine.

"You didn't."

"I sure did!"

"Betty!"

Jennifer shakes her head as she takes a sip. Her stomach growls loudly. They both laugh. Jennifer admires her friend's fun, if not outrageous, style. Always colorful, with full hair and makeup.

The waiter grins. "Would you like to order?"

"Uh, yeah," Jennifer giggles, embarrassed. "I'll have a cheeseburger. Rare. With fries."

He turns to Betty. "Ma'am?"

"I'll have the grilled chicken salad. Ranch on the side, please."

The waiter takes the menus and heads for the kitchen.

"Betty, I really shouldn't drink. It's the middle of the day."

"Come on."

"Oh, fine. I'll sacrifice."

"You seem a lot better than you sounded this morning," Betty says invitingly.

"I know. It's part of my psychotic existence." Jennifer takes another sip of wine. "Okay, this was a good call. Thank you for meeting me. And I'm really sorry I was late."

"My pleasure, and don't worry. I'm glad you're here."

Jennifer takes a huge bite of brie. "I don't know what the hell I'm doing," she says with her mouth full. "I think I'm losing it."

"Why?"

"I feel like there's two of me."

"Well," Betty's concern is genuine. "How are things since you moved out?"

"I absolutely love my apartment. And there's something about the process, decorating it, that feels amazing. Important. I was never into that with James. And it's fun! In fact, I need to stop at the store later today and see if I can get some pillows. And maybe a plant."

"Good for you! I bet it looks great."

"It's getting there."

Jennifer looks off into the distance, remembering their recent therapy session.

"What?" Betty asks.

"I don't know. Just thinking about James."

"How so?"

"I can't stand him. But . . . what he's got, that no one else does, is he's the father of my children. Otherwise, we'd already be divorced."

"You sure?"

Jennifer stares hard at her friend. "Yes. There was a second, maybe just half a second the other day, where I didn't know. I felt like maybe I should try to make it work . . ." She pauses to sip. "But that just pissed me off."

"I don't think I could stay." Betty shakes her head. "And the other guy?"

"I realized something about him, just before I came here. Actually, it's more about me."

"Yeah?"

"There's something in me that flips. Like when I'm with him, I'm not sure. And then when I think about what it would be like for real—" She drifts for a moment back to the shower, then bed. "I've only told him I love him when we're having sex."

"You sound like a man." Betty smirks.

Jennifer makes a face. "Thanks."

"Go on."

"It's something—like when I'm away from him, I don't trust him. And when he's there, I don't have a real sense of him. I can't tell who he is. But we go somewhere . . . when we—okay, this is really—I feel like an idiot. I don't know what I'm trying to say."

"What? Where do you go? Really. I really want to know."

"It's—" Jennifer searches. "It feels like touching God. Sounds crazy, but it's white there. Silent. That's the place where I love him. So, I feel terrible, because I don't even know if it's him, or something in me, that I'm loving. The experience itself."

"Who cares!"

"And he's starting to want something more. I just don't know."

"Tell him you need time."

"I do. I mean, I'm still in therapy with James. I'm doing this back-and-forth in my head. It's awful."

The waiter appears and sets their food on the table. "More wine?"

Jennifer realizes her glass is almost empty. "No, but water would be great. And coffee in a bit, please."

"Me too," says Betty.

Jennifer dives into her burger. It's just what she needs.

"You know, Jen," Betty teases, "maybe you should send this guy my way."

Jennifer laughs loudly. "Good one."

"Have I ever seen him?"

Jennifer shakes her head. "It's for your own good."

"I know, I know. Is he tall?"

"Tall enough. He's not the typical kind of handsome. But it's . . . it's the energy." Jennifer looks at her watch. "Time flies when you're in complete confusion."

Betty looks at her friend. "What do you want?"

"I don't know. Everything! I want this person as a lover. I want my children to live with their mom and dad. I want to go back and not have married James." Jennifer chokes up. "But I love Jimmy and Chloe."

"Oh, don't worry, Jen." Betty places her hand over Jennifer's. "They're gonna be okay. You're the best mom I know."

"I don't feel like it. I'm afraid the right thing for everyone else is not the right thing for me. How do I deal with that?"

"You do the best you can." Betty squeezes her hand.

"I'm trying so hard to figure it out." Hot tears spill down Jennifer's cheeks. She brings the cloth napkin to her face.

"Jen, take it easy on yourself. It'll take time."

"I know."

"Coffee?" The waiter is back.

"I—" says Jennifer. "I'll be right back." She feels light-headed as she walks toward the back of the restaurant, like moving through dense fog. In the bathroom, Jennifer splashes cold water on her face. She checks herself in the mirror. Her eyes are puffy. Her hair, rumpled. She pulls it quickly back in a knot and dries her face. She looks about eighteen somehow in the lighting. She feels eighty.

Back at the table, Jennifer is thankful for the coffee. She sips it, grateful for the rich flavor and caffeine.

"Whatever you decide, Jen, know that I'm here. Call me anytime. For anything."

Jennifer nods.

"I'm serious." Betty pats Jennifer's wrist.

"I know. Thank you so much. I'm sure I will. I feel like I have so far to go."

"Are you going to see him again?"

Jennifer laughs. "Which one?"

"Either." Betty chuckles.

"James at drop-off and therapy next week. The other? What am I going to do? I'd see him. That's the thing. If he calls. Even if I don't want to."

Kate

Nothing is working. Kate has been crying for weeks. The house is a mess. There's laundry everywhere, clean piles now spilling into the dirty piles. She hasn't washed a dish in days. She avoids David—worried if she speaks, she will destroy him. Only Peter and Ben pull her to the immediacy of the present.

"Mom, have you seen my shoes lately?" Kate looks to see a gaping hole at the top of Peter's left shoe, and another beginning on his right.

"I'm sorry, Peter." She sighs. "Let's get you some new shoes after school today."

"Me too!" Ben jumps in.

"Yours, my dear, look perfectly fine."

"But I want new shoes too!" he insists.

"Okay, if we can find some on sale." Kate turns back to Peter, who never asks for anything new. "Why didn't you tell me? I feel awful you've been wearing those."

"I didn't want to make you mad."

"Mad?"

"Yeah . . . ," Peter speaks tentatively. "Seems like you're mad all the time. Or sad."

Kate feels an intense stomach pang. "Oh, Peter. I'm just going through some things lately. I'm really, really sorry. Please, always know you can talk to me. No matter what."

"I know. I didn't really care, anyway," he says, looking down at his shoe. "Then I tripped on it in gym." He smiles.

"I love you, honey." Kate pulls him close.

"I love you too." Peter hugs her back.

"Group hug!" Ben comes out of nowhere, knocking them both to the floor. Kate looks at her boys as they laugh together, sprawled out on the ground. They are fine. She is not.

She can tell David wishes she would attend to him the way she does with the boys. She wants him to stand strong. Be a real partner. She sees that for years David has been "jumping into the basket" (one of many Marta-isms) with Peter and Ben, to be mothered and nurtured by her.

Marta understood and had helped put it into words. She didn't tell her to keep doing what she's been doing. She validated Kate's need for David to take care of himself, energetically and emotionally. "He is a grown-up," Marta had said.

Kate doesn't have it in her anymore. She has spent all these years trying to make up for the hurt he incurred in childhood. She has offered David a kind of emotional caretaking that isn't healthy for either one of them.

Something is changing.

Maybe it would be easier to move out. Have her own little place. Kate questions what it's like for children to divide their time between two households. Does that external split become internalized for them?

Peter's shoes. She must remember.

)))

"Why are you so angry with me?" David lies staring at the ceiling.

Unlike with Peter, she is.

"Are you?" he asks.

"Yeah." She said it.

"Why? What did I do?" He is up on his elbow, looking at Kate. Now she's the one staring at the ceiling.

"It's . . . everything. I don't know."

"You don't know what?"

"If—" Kate looks directly at him. Deep breath. "If I want to be married."

David lets out a huge sigh. "Because of what?"

"Now you sound angry."

"I am! What the hell is this about? Are you seeing someone?"

"No. I'm not."

Kate thinks about the massage she had last week and how she cried as she felt her body screaming, deep within her belly, for a man who knew how to be with her.

"You sure?" David asks.

"Yes." She feels a remove. From herself. "How about you?"

"What?"

"You seeing anyone?"

Kate wants to be brave enough to ask what she's wanted to for so long. Have you? Ever?

"Why are you asking me this?" he asks.

"Because you're completely unavailable. We hardly ever have sex." The hurt and humiliation run deep. "And you look at other women. Even when I'm with you." David looks away. "You're not at all who I thought you were," she says.

"Neither are you," he quips.

"Can you just listen a minute? You come home late. Are on your computer constantly—playing games, watching porn."

"No, I'm not!"

"Yes, you are!" Kate is furious. "Don't lie."

David says nothing.

"Well?" she demands.

Nothing.

"There are two people in this relationship. Feels like you're not even here." Kate gets up and begins pulling on a pair of jeans. "That's how I've felt our entire marriage," she continues. "What difference would it make if we separated? You're never here, David! Even when you are, you're not." She grabs a sweatshirt from the closet, sliding it over her head. "Why did I even marry you?" Her heart pounds. Is she screaming?

"You seriously want to separate?" asks David.

"You were so different then."

"Do you?"

Kate looks at him. "I hate what your mother did to you. How she hurt you and made something in you . . . so absent. I can't overcome that. I thought I could."

David continues to lie there. No response.

Kate suddenly can't stay in the room with him another moment. "Don't forget to give the boys breakfast," she calls over her shoulder. "They've been dying for some time with you. Especially Peter. I'll be back in a few hours."

)))

KATE FINDS HERSELF WALKING TOWARD THE PARK. SHE CRIES, longing for the feeling of holding her babies' little bodies. She used to have the power to make everything all right. Or is it herself she wants to hold? She had finally confronted David. And he didn't answer. Didn't say a real word.

Tired, Kate sits on a bench. Sun pours over her. The warmth slowly begins to calm her, reminding her she is one tiny piece of this world. Her mind slowly settles. Her heartbeat finds its natural rhythm. Kate moves into an almost eerie calm.

After what feels like a long while, she stands and continues her walk. She has never gone this way before. Kate follows a narrow path, down some steps, and heads toward a wooded area.

Then she sees him. A little boy, standing by a tree. All alone. His eyes are big and blue. Kate looks around.

"Is there a grown-up with you?"

He doesn't speak.

"I know you don't know me," she continues, "but I'm a safe person to help you find your mom or dad."

"My mama." His voice is darling. Scared.

"Okay. Let's find her. Did you come from over there?" Kate points. "The playground?"

He nods. She carefully takes his tiny hand in hers, and they walk toward the park. A woman runs in the distance, looking panicked.

"He's over here!" Kate yells.

The woman runs to them. "Sweetheart!" She throws her arms around the boy, pulling him to her. "Oh my God, where were you, sweetie? Mama was so worried." Her hands shake as she turns to Kate. "Where was he?"

Kate's heart skips a beat, as though she knows this woman. But how?

"Over there," she answers. "In the woods. He seemed fine when I found him. Just scared."

"You okay?" She takes his face in her hands, kissing him. He nods and buries his head in her shoulder. The woman turns to Kate. "Thank you!"

"No one was with him," Kate reassures her. "I think he's okay."

"You stay with Mama. Always." She scoops her little boy up in her arms. Then pauses, her cheeks flushed. "I was with my daughter and a friend. I thought . . . my friend doesn't have kids . . . and I thought she was watching him. But she wasn't. Thank you. I don't know how to thank you."

Kate remembers a time, years ago, when she was at the park with a friend, and Peter ran off while they were talking. She searched everywhere. By the time she found him, she was a wreck. It's impossible not to think of what might have happened.

"Come, sweet boy. Thank you," the woman says again. She turns and walks with him back to the playground, where her friend and daughter are waiting. They gather up their belongings and head to the parking lot. Kate watches them the whole way. As the woman opens the rear car door and places the boy in his car seat, it hits her. Kate is astonished.

SPLIT OPEN

Never has a stranger been so familiar. Everything feels suddenly light.

The dream had been over a year ago—yet was still so vivid. How is it possible? She was here? Real? In Evanston? Not floating through an imaginary party. She had real issues and problems. Had she had an affair? Had her husband? Were they really separated, like Kate wants to separate from David?

Does she?

As that thought comes, Kate notices the strangest thing. She is no longer angry. She can't feel her rage. She searches her head. Stomach. Heart. There's only emptiness.

Then gratitude. This morning she was in the exact right place at the exact right time. Ben was that little boy's age not long ago and had a similar look. Kate would bury her nose in his hair, breathe him in. He called her *Mama* too.

Her feet on the ground, Kate begins to walk, one step at a time, back home. When she opens the back door, David is washing dishes. His eyes are timid.

"You have a good walk?"

"Yeah, I did. I needed that." Kate suddenly feels so heavy. "I'm exhausted."

"I'll take the boys to a movie or something," he offers. "You need a break."

"I do. Where are they?"

"PlayStation."

"I'll go say hi. Then I have to lie down." She can hardly stand.

"Whatever you need."

"Right now, I really need a nap." Now he decides to show up? Kate is aware there is a choice. We can either identify with and grasp the things we own and have—what is tangible—or, we can strive for something beyond our view, outside of our knowing. The unseen. Her internal response is immediate. Unwavering. She feels her inner self reach out, into the unknown. Running—with the intent to fly.

Suddenly, she feels as though she is leaping out of the top of her head, flying into the sky. Fearless! Everything is vivid, colors intenser than ever. She rolls and turns in the air. Joyful, free, and fully herself. It's freezing, and the cold spreads slowly from her back toward her middle. Chilling her core. Her hair whips in the wind, the sound almost deafening. She has never felt this alive!

A cough. Kate is simultaneously in two places at once, then back in her body. On the bed. She opens her eyes. Ben stands, staring at her. As she smiles at him, Kate realizes her back is still cold, even though she lies under three heavy blankets. Was she dreaming?

Jennifer

"Mama!" Jennifer sits upright. "Mama!" She runs to Jimmy's room. He is twisted in his blanket, tears running down his cheeks.

"It's okay. It's okay. Shhhh . . . Mama's here."

"Mama! I lost you. There was grass and trees and—"

She holds her little boy, soothingly rocking him. "It's okay," she repeats. Jimmy quickly falls back to sleep, Jennifer wrapped around him. She lies with him, squeezed onto his bed, holding him close. She lies awake as he sleeps. Tomorrow, she must take Jimmy and Chloe to James's. It doesn't feel right to be routinely separated from her young children. Not even for two nights. Her stomach clinches.

Jennifer imagines James in a car accident. Dead. The children would be devastated. They would have no father. She would feel for them and her own sadness. But it would be out of her control. A tragic accident. Fate. They would cry hard at his funeral. How many people would be there? Probably a lot. Many she wouldn't know, through his business. But they would know of her. They would give their condolences. She would mourn the loss of him. And the loss of what was gone long ago.

Chloe and Jimmy would be with her.

Jennifer shakes her head. She needs to sleep. She feels so vulnerable sometimes in the night. Made of thin glass. Fear and upset roaming through the corners of her mind.

The alarm from her own room sounds. For a moment, Jennifer is disoriented. Jimmy sleeps next to her. She carefully gets up, runs to her room, and turns off the loud beeping. She hurries into the shower. Her mind slips into the memory of her shower with Andrew. His hands . . .

Anger wells up in response to her longing. How is this getting her anywhere? She can't imagine marrying him. Then again, who says she wants to be married? To anyone? She wants the security of marriage, yes. But not the trappings. It's terrible to feel owned.

Jennifer turns off the water and dries herself. She looks in the mirror. Through the fog, she seems insubstantial, as though she's not really there. She has lost weight. Stress. She knows she's running on empty. But there is no other way. She must continue to move through this. For her children. She must come to some place of understanding with James. "It's the doing of it that makes it real," she tells her reflection. If words are not made real through action, they are worthless. Just like her marriage. Just like her hopes and dreams.

☾ ☾ ☾

"Here's your oatmeal." Jennifer hands a bowl to Jimmy. Her baby—so big and so little. Tears sting her eyes. She hardly feels like herself.

"More brown sugar," Jimmy demands.

"Okay, a little." She yells towards the bathroom, "Chloe?"

"Coming!"

"Come on, sweetie. We need to leave in ten minutes."

Jennifer holds on to the hope that the more she is able to wrestle with her personal demons, the more it will benefit her daughter. She will not pass down to Chloe what she received from her own mother. Her mother didn't love herself. Or feel at home. Especially when she was at home with Jennifer.

"Here, sweetheart." Jennifer hands Chloe a bowl.

"I'm not really hungry."

"Eat half of it. Please." Jennifer longs to hold her. Protect her. Care for her. Make everything okay. Just go back to James, maybe, so Chloe will be okay.

"Fine."

"Good," Jennifer continues. "You and I need to figure out some girl time. When you come back from Daddy's. Okay?"

Chloe looks at her. "We go today, right?"

"Yeah. I'll pick you up from school and take you over there at five thirty."

"Mama? How many days?" How could Jimmy possibly grasp this concept, even after months?

"Two." She holds up two fingers. "Two nights sleeping at

Daddy's house, then I'll come get you and bring you back to Mommy's house."

"'Kay," he says, seemingly unfazed.

Is he really all right? Or is this affecting him in ways that won't show up for years? Is Jennifer fundamentally damaging her children? The thought is horrifying. The option is to stop, give up her apartment, and move back in with James. The family would be together again. But at what cost?

"Let's brush teeth quickly and get our shoes on. Time to go." If only the separation impacted her alone. "You circled you want school lunch today, Chloe. And Jimmy? You have a string cheese, crackers, and grapes in your lunch box. Eat it. Okay?"

"How about juice?" he asks.

"Yes, juice. But eat your food too. At least the string cheese."

Jennifer drops Chloe at school and heads toward Jimmy's preschool. She decides to touch base quickly with his teacher. Her conference with Chloe's teacher is scheduled for the end of the week. Jennifer wonders about her children's lives away from her. Do things show up in their behavior at school that she doesn't know about? Are they going to be okay?

Kate

"I've been in my writing circle for three weeks," Kate shares.

"How is it?" Marta has her hair tied back. She is striking.

"Really good. Different from any class I've ever taken."

David takes in the room. "She's always in a good mood when she gets back."

It feels strange to have David in Marta's office. Surprising he even came.

"I brought a poem I wrote last class. It showed me something, about where I am. I can't really explain." Kate looks at Marta. "Can I read it?"

"Of course."

"It's for David." Kate opens the letter.

"*David.*"

She looks at him, then back to her paper. Heart racing.

"I want to fall in love with you again. To laugh with you, be embraced by you. I long to feel my heart captured by the mere sight of you. Choose me. Cherish me."

She stops. Remembering her breath, Kate finds her voice again. *"Look into me, past tired angry woman, past mother, and dreams that might have been. Spill into the depths of me, rocking, knocking me over—till I fall—fall over, onto you, into you. Catch me. Comfort me. And I will do the same for you. Share your deepest thoughts with me. Open yourself. Don't pull away. There's nothing to fear. I've been waiting so long for you to Unwrap me."*

Kate's throat is tight. She looks up. David has tears in his eyes. After a long silence, Marta speaks, "David? What are you feeling right now?"

"It's . . . beautiful." His voice becomes almost a whisper. "And I'm surprised."

"How so?" asks Marta.

"I thought Kate was going to tell me she wanted out. I thought that's why she brought me here."

"I think . . . I was. When I asked you to come," Kate says softly. "I don't really know what I want, honestly. I feel split."

"She's been angry all of a sudden." David sounds vulnerable.

"All of a sudden?" Kate feels stung.

"And acting so emotional. She's all over the place."

"David," suggests Marta, "can you speak directly to Kate?"

David turns to face Kate. His eyes well up again. "I have no idea what to do." He pauses, looking down at his hands. "I feel like you see me as damaged goods . . ." He can barely get the words out. "Which I am." He reaches for a tissue and brings it to his nose. "I've just been waiting for the next shoe to drop."

"David?" Marta speaks so tenderly. "How do you feel about Kate?"

"I think she's a wonderful mother. I think it's good she's writing; I can tell it makes her happy." He pauses. "But I—" David searches. "I don't know what she wants."

"What do *you* want?" Kate asks him.

"Our family," David answers.

"Do you want *me*?" Her stomach is knotted up.

"Of course. I always have."

"You sure have a strange way of showing it!"

Marta looks at Kate. "Can you say more?"

"He—"

"Can you say it right to David?" Marta reminds her.

Kate looks at her husband. He looks familiar, yet different. "I feel like we live in the same space, but our lives are so separate. *You* are separate. You don't even see us."

"Us?" he asks.

"Don't get mad. I'm saying what I feel." Kate sighs and looks at Marta. "The longer I'm married to him, the more I feel David's relationship with his mother, growing up, has to do with his absence in our relationship—and with Peter and Ben."

"Peter and Ben?" David looks stunned.

"Are you serious?"

"I'm a good dad."

"You are a good dad—when you're paying attention. You have no idea how much I cover for you. How often they—especially Peter—how he comes to me so sad. Needing you."

"What do you mean?" David sounds confused.

"There are times he talks to you and you're so checked out, you literally don't hear him. Then he comes to me, and I find a way to use humor to help bring him perspective about you—and make sure he doesn't personalize it as a rejection." Kate pauses. "It happens a lot."

"I . . . I have no idea what you're talking about."

"I know you don't." She looks away.

"Well, what do you want me to do?" he asks.

"Wake up!"

"David," Marta interrupts, "I wonder if the first step is to simply begin to bring awareness to what Kate is saying. She's talking about your relationship with your mother and also your son. Do you hear her?"

"I do, but honestly, I feel like I'm there. Why does she think I'm not?"

"Perhaps the way of being there that you are used to is different from the way she is asking you to be—both with her and the children."

David looks perplexed.

"It is not a matter of right or wrong," Marta continues. "There are different ways to be with one another. It's possible that your way of existing in your childhood home is one way of being. And she is asking to be met another way."

"How?"

"With presence," Marta says gently.

"How do I do that?" David sounds genuine.

"It will not be easy. It will take time. For now, awareness is good. Very important."

"What does that look like?" asks Kate.

"I'm not sure," Marta responds. "There's a lot going on here."

Kate can't imagine how anything could ever really change. Every time she had thought things were different, it didn't hold. He—they—returned to the same patterns. "How are we supposed to be? With each other?" she asks. "When we're at home?"

"Well . . ." Marta thinks for a moment. "It could be that in the past, the two of you were a certain way. Maybe as you continue to do your own work and find a life independent from your wifing and mothering, the relationship is being asked to change. Maybe as you explore who you are, the marriage is in a place of transition. Do you think it is possible to just hold there and not know right now?"

David leans back in his chair, crossing his arms.

Marta turns to him. "What are you thinking?"

"I mean, I'll do whatever," he says. "I . . . I don't want to be nonpresent."

Marta looks at Kate. "How do you feel?"

"I'm not sure." Kate feels the tension she's been holding for so long, both wanting to save her marriage and leave it. "Part of me wants to work on this. But honestly . . ." She leans forward, allowing her head to fall into her hands. "Part of me feels it's too late. I'm so angry. And hurt."

Marta responds, "Maybe the split you feel, and that David is hearing from you, is important. It could be coming up so you have the opportunity to see it and work with it. Bring awareness to it."

"It's getting really confusing," Kate says.

"Can you simply let it be there—both the rage you are feeling and the love you have for one another? You have two wonderful boys who make it worthwhile to move slowly with this."

Kate nods. Marta turns her attention to David. "Are you willing for the relationship to hold some changes? Especially as Kate moves a bit more into life outside of wife and mother?"

"Yes."

"I think her writing is important," Marta says.

"I think so too." David seems raw. "She writes more from her heart than anyone I've ever known. My process is very different."

"And you are a writer too?"

David and Kate look at each other and smile. He is an accomplished writer, highly paid and regarded. But Marta makes Kate feel no less important.

"Yes," he answers.

"I think a person's creative work is the most important thing," Marta responds. "It's clear that Kate is a creative person, and I think it is essential for her to bring her questions, all that she is going through, into her creative process. Otherwise, it might eat you both alive."

David and Kate nod.

"Sometimes it feels like too much," says Kate. "I feel like I can't do it all."

"I'm not stopping you." David is still.

"But you're frightened of me. I can see it in your eyes. Like you don't know who I am."

"Sometimes I don't."

"I can't make things comfortable for you and, at the same time, find myself."

SPLIT OPEN

Marta steps in. "I think, David, Kate needs to know you are willing to take care of yourself in this. She can't move forward with her life and not rock the boat a bit."

"I don't want to be responsible for your well-being, if that makes sense," Kate tells him. "And will you find someone of your own, a therapist, to work with? I need to know that you're really going to do what you say you will. Because you so often don't."

David looks like he's about to say something, then stops himself. "Yes," he answers.

"If you need a recommendation," Marta offers, "I can give you the names of a few male therapists, all of whom are extraordinarily deep and sensitive. I think any one of them would be a good fit for you."

As they walk to the car, David reaches for Kate's hand. She allows him to take it.

"I'm glad you came today," she says.

"Me too."

"I'm so hungry."

"What do you feel like?"

"A burger!" Kate feels suddenly ravenous.

"Let's get one." David smiles. "Kate, I support you, I really do."

"My writing is really important to me. My dreams too."

"Good." David leans in and kisses her softly on the lips. Kate begins to cry.

"Happy tears?"

"Yeah."

"Just checking." David pulls her close.

Jennifer

"You want to have dinner?" Andrew's voice is hypnotic.

"I don't know. Maybe," Jennifer tentatively answers.

"Come on, baby. How about you get dressed up and I'll come pick you up."

"Maybe you should just come over."

"I will, if that's what you want . . ." Andrew pauses. "But you could use some fun. Let me take you out, like a real couple."

That stops her cold. She doesn't feel like a real couple. She doesn't want to. She isn't divorced yet and isn't completely sure.

"We'll have a few drinks," he continues, "go dancing. How 'bout it?"

Jennifer exhales heavily.

"Jennifer, baby." Andrew holds his patient tone. "What is it you want?"

"I'm scared."

"I know you are. You're scared about everything. But I'm the one thing that won't hurt you. Let's put some pleasure in the world. You want me to come over?"

She wants him badly. She feels overwhelming heat between her legs. "Yeah."

"Okay. When?" Andrew asks.

"Now."

"I'll be right there. Maybe dinner after. We'll see how you feel."

Everything is gone but the desire she feels. Jennifer doesn't want to think anymore. She wants to hide with him, under the covers, behind closed doors.

She runs a brush through her hair and decides to put on something nice. She wants to please him. Searching her underwear drawer, she finds her light, see-through short slip. He'll like this one. As Jennifer slides it over her head, she feels herself transforming.

A knock.

She quickly swirls mouthwash, spits it out, then glances in the mirror. Sometimes there is a kind of fragile, ephemeral beauty she recognizes in herself. As if all pretense has been stripped away and she stares directly into her core.

Andrew's arms are around her the second she opens the door. He kisses her deeply. Runs his hands over her breasts. Then takes a step back to look at her.

"Very nice." He smiles. "You should wear this all day, every day, wherever you go."

Jennifer laughs. She knows he means it.

He strokes her hair. "You want to talk, baby? What do you need?"

"This," she answers. She runs her tongue over his lips and into his mouth. She pushes her body to his, feeling his chest, his arms, his back.

"God, you're sexy," he purrs. Jennifer continues to kiss him. She moves her hands along his back, scratching with her fingernails.

"I need you."

Andrew's energy grows until it matches her intensity. They begin their dance. There's no restaurant. No people. No music.

)))

Andrew kisses her forehead, then slowly strokes her cheek. "Jennifer, what do you want?"

She emerges from a foggy half sleep. "Hmm?"

"You don't want to go out anywhere with me. You want me to come make love to you, which is great. It's—" Andrew seems more vulnerable than usual. "But it's my only way into you. Besides that, you're shut down."

Jennifer stares at the ceiling. At the breakable light cover. She should smash it.

"What do you want from me?" he presses.

"I . . . It changes. I don't know."

"Well, don't you think it's a little unfair? I have to pry you open between your legs?"

"I don't know what I'm doing."

"Well, why can't you just love me? Be with me?" Andrew rolls on top of her and holds her face in his hands. "Nobody will ever love you like I do. I'm the right man for you."

Jennifer kisses him, bringing her arms around him, pressing her hands into his back.

"See? That's your only response. Here I'm telling you I love you and you want to have sex again." He pulls away abruptly. "What is it with you?"

Jennifer has no answer. She feels ashamed. What Andrew's saying is true.

"How about you call me when you want to see me and go out with me. I can't keep doing this. I mean, I will. I can't resist you. I'll have sex with you probably for the rest of my life if you call. But I just can't do this right now." He has moved from the bed and is pulling on his pants and shirt.

Jennifer feels hot shame and fear and need. No words come to her. She watches him button his shirt and start to put on his socks and shoes.

"Do you love me?" Andrew asks.

She is curled in a ball.

He moves to her. "Do you want to be with me?"

Why isn't she stopping him? If she just said it, just told him she wanted him, he wouldn't leave.

Andrew stands. "I don't want to go. I don't want to leave you like this. I'm madly in love with you. I love you more than anyone in my life. Jennifer. Look at me."

She does.

"What do you want?"

Why can't she speak?

Jennifer watches as Andrew turns and slowly leaves the room. There were tears in his eyes. She saw them. She hears the front door open, senses him standing in the doorway for a long time . . . Then, quietly, the door shuts.

YEAR THREE

OPENING

Kate

"I love you, honey."

Peter makes a face, then breaks into a full smile. "You too, Mom." He has cream cheese on his cheek and a hot chocolate mustache.

Peter has grown incredibly with this move. His attachment to his old friends, his love of Ojai, and his specific personality made the transition difficult for him. He needs order, routine, and consistency. The move had made him feel intensely displaced. And anxious.

Peter also went through a huge change when Ben was born. What a major life transition. David was unavailable, both physically and emotionally. That whole year had an underwater, nightmarish quality to it. There were times Kate was so hungry and would lie on the couch and cry, unable even to make a sandwich.

She felt guilty about that year, especially regarding Peter. He went from having her devoted attention to having a stressed-out mess of a mother. As she looks at him, Kate realizes that she has, with this move, given Peter back that year. She made supporting his emotional stability a priority.

Ben didn't need much the first year in Evanston, but Peter had regressed. He desperately wanted to feel safe. She had held him through his pain, never asking him to be more okay than he was.

"You remember that field trip?" she asks. "In Ojai?"

"What field trip?"

"The one to the Santa Barbara Mission?"

"Oh yeah, we made that cool model of it."

"Exactly." Kate smiles. She had gotten a little too into that art project. For some reason, she couldn't help herself. Especially the detailed clay roof tile.

"And the Ojai Trolley!"

Peter and Ben loved the Ojai Trolley. For another school project, they all worked together cutting and transforming a big box into the cutest Ojai Trolley, using red and green paint. The boys were little enough back then that they could play in it. One of Kate's favorite photos is of them peeking out of an imperfectly cut window.

"Do you miss Ojai?" asks Kate.

Peter thinks for a moment. "No. I did, but I'm so glad we moved here."

He made a handful of close friends that first year in Evanston. They seemed to have real loyalty to one another and were highly creative in their play.

"I'm done," Peter says, pushing his plate away. "Can we go? I want to see if Bobby's home." His best friend.

"Absolutely. Here." Kate hands Peter a napkin. "The right side, on your cheek."

Peter wipes away the cream cheese, and they head out of the coffee shop to the parking lot. Kate starts the car.

"You're a special boy." Challenging. Magical. "I'm so glad you're my son."

"I'm glad you're my mom."

Kate pulls out of their parking space.

"Mom?"

"Yeah?"

"Remember at the Santa Barbara Mission, how you got on the school bus?"

Kate's heart beats fast. Why had she and Peter never talked about it? "I sure do. What do you remember?"

"It was like flashes." Peter and his whole class watched it happen. "You were like a superhero."

Tears well up and fall quickly down Kate's cheeks.

"Why are you crying?"

"I . . ." Kate smiles at Peter in the rearview mirror. "I hadn't really thought about what it was like for you to see."

"Yeah." Peter looks out the window. "It was really cool."

◗ ● ●

"Hey!" Nia waves, already at the trail as Kate pulls in.

"Hey!" She gets out of her car.

"You'll never guess who is back in Evanston."

"Who?"

"Joseph Johnson."

"From high school?"

"Not only is he back," Nia continues, "he's a professor of chemistry at Northwestern."

"No!"

"Yes." They begin to walk at a nice pace. "I ran into him on campus. I mean, literally. I was turning a corner and ran smack-dab into him, Kate. Literally."

"Literally?"

"Literally!" They both start laughing.

"What happened?"

"We just started talking. Like no time had passed. I had to teach, so we made plans and met after work."

"What? He asked you out?"

"It wasn't like that"—Nia smiles—"at first, anyway."

"Tell me everything!"

"You will not believe where we went."

"Where?"

"We ended up going to the Moon Room! It's still there and is exactly the same—even the corner booth in the back."

"The best one!"

"And that's where we sat!" Nia's excitement grows.

"Are our initials still on the wall?"

"Yes!"

"Unbelievable!"

"Oh my gosh, Kate, it was like time stood still and flew by. We ordered, and talked, and laughed, and ended up ordering again we were there for so long, just talking. And we ended up getting close enough to ask the big question of *what ever happened to us?*"

"Are you kidding?"

Nia looks breathless. Is it the fast walking pace or her enthusiasm about Joseph? "I couldn't believe it. Here we are, after all these years, and we're scarfing down food in front of each other, during a time when most people would be trying to put their best foot forward, and we didn't have anything to prove to one another. It was absolutely amazing. When we got to that point of asking what happened to us, Kate, I don't know." Nia takes a breath. "It's like we were just so focused that summer on making our families proud and going to our undergraduate colleges across the country from one another . . . and making sure we didn't waste our chance to have an opportunity at these degrees. And yeah, when we got there, we dated people off and on, just like people do in college. And even during grad school, we would check in with each other, but not directly." Nia laughs and rolls her eyes. "We were too shy to do that. We would actually check on each other through mutual friends. It seems like we were both afraid to hear that we were happy with other people, and we didn't want the other one to know we were checking in."

"My mind is blown right now." Kate's jaw is wide open.

"Oh my gosh." Nia holds her head in her two hands. "I can't believe that we were both feeling the same thing at the same time, while finishing one degree, going to the next graduate degree, even starting our doctorate degrees, and wondering if each other were thinking about getting married to the person that we imagined them with. All of this was in our heads. As it turns out, neither of us was even thinking about getting married! He told me he couldn't ever marry somebody that he wasn't in love with. He wasn't ever going to settle. It's funny, I've always had that same feeling—why settle?"

Kate, in her mind and her stomach, can't believe how right everything feels about what Nia is saying. If only . . .

They come to a downhill part of the trail, their pace slowing. Nia keeps talking as if she were still back in the Moon Room, reflecting.

"You might not remember, because you were pretty involved with the fellowship at the time, but I grew up in an AME church down on Roosevelt Street. It was a pretty small church at the time, and my family's been in it for years. You won't believe this part, Kate. Fast-forward to now, where we are right now, and guess who goes to that church?"

"No!"

"Yes! And he started going after he got back to Evanston. I had no idea because the church has grown after all these years and has all these outreach ministries where it's actually pretty easy to not know that he was there. As it turns out, he's been tutoring, volunteering to help kids with math and science on the weekends."

What would it be like to be with a man like that? Kate imagines Joseph tutoring a child, just because it's a good thing to do. She can't help contrasting that with David, who wouldn't even hold on to Peter's hand when she told him to. They could have lost Peter. Her stomach turns over.

"And, Kate," Nia continues, "you can never imagine what the cutest thing is . . ."

"I can't imagine anything cuter than what you've already said! What? Tell me!"

"He doesn't just tutor, he also promised this one kid to go to his Little League games. Can you believe that?"

Kate remembers Joseph from high school. They were all kids back then. But to hear how Joseph has evolved into being a real man that shows up with such selfless responsibility and care for others . . . "If anyone deserves to have someone this well rounded, it's you, Nia. I *can* believe it."

Nia grabs Kate's hand and squeezes. Kate squeezes back. "I have a good feeling about him, Kate. He's intelligent, attractive, and I can already tell we share the same values—the big three."

"The big three?"

"The most important thing for me to agree on with anyone is who we worship, so we have the same belief in the Lord. Next, on one of those fat juicy burgers we were chomping down on, we ended up talking about kids . . . and it came up so naturally, Kate, because we were talking about the child he tutors from Little League. And he was talking about how much he really admires the boy's parents and how they're raising him. I absolutely loved that!"

"What's the third?"

"The third one," Nia answers, "is money."

"Ah! Of course."

Kate's mind is spinning. Why hadn't she thought about things like this? She and David never discussed values and compatibility when they were dating. They were drawn to each other and just went with it.

"Okay, I have to ask, with no pun intended . . ." Kate grins mischievously. "How's the *chemistry*?"

"Palpable."

They grin at one another.

"You're beaming!"

"Am I?"

Kate laughs, knowing Nia is fully aware of her glow. It's been such a long time since Kate felt that way.

"I really like him." Nia giggles.

"You sound about sixteen!"

"I feel like I am!"

Kate bursts with joy for her friend—then feels something else. She looks at the trees. So tall. Graceful. She wants to leap out of her skin. Into Nia's life. "You honestly deserve every bit of this. When are you seeing him again?"

"Joseph asked me out for dinner this Saturday."

"This is phenomenal!" Kate turns her face upward. Soothing sun. The trees seem to shimmer, tiny buds sprouting everywhere. Why had she fallen so quickly for David? Why the rush? Her friends who married later in life seemed to choose more appropriate partners. They were more formed. Knew who they were. A playful tap on her shoulder. "What?"

"Daydreaming beauty."

"You're the beauty! I'm over the moon for you, Nia. You and Joseph!"

"Me too. He said it's a surprise where he's taking me and to wear something nice. I think this warrants a shopping trip!"

"I'm already there. You just say when and where. You're going to be gorgeous." The Moon Room. Wow . . . "Joseph and Nia, all grown up, back in the back booth."

"Life is good." They walk in silence for a bit. "How are you and David?" asks Nia.

"Hmm . . ." The fresh air feels invigorating. "Interesting."

"Meaning?"

"We went to see Marta together."

"What was that like?"

"Hard. Good. Surprising. I'm finally starting to feel like the main character in my own story." Kate lets out a hearty laugh. "That's a Marta-ism."

"Oh, I love that!"

"It's taken long enough."

"You've been raising your children. The timing is good."

"And"—Kate hesitates for just a moment—"my writing seems to be turning into a novel."

"Wow! A novel! That's wonderful."

Kate imagines a scene between two new lovers exploring each other's bodies for the first time. And then simply being together, enjoying one another's company. "I'm so happy for you, Nia." Kate says as she puts her arm around her friend. "You're really something."

☽ ● ●

"It was intense. I was suddenly aware there was a wild animal in the house. A black jaguar! And she was growing bigger. Dangerous. I was terrified she might kill and eat us—and also terrified of letting her out of the house because of what she might do." Kate realizes her shoulders are creeping up toward her ears. "That was it, the whole dream. It's like it happened in an instant. What do you think?"

"What do *you* think?" Marta hands the question back to Kate.

"I don't know. I woke up completely panicked."

"Jaguars can be a symbol of true power," Marta offers. "You may be in the process of reclaiming the power within yourself."

Kate nods.

Marta continues, "This creature may be speaking to the deep creative place of darkness. Of night—specifically representing the divine feminine. Mother. Moon. Creation."

"Wow."

Marta looks at her bookshelf, then back to Kate. "Do you have an animal book?"

"Like what?" Kate has no idea.

"That explains their meaning? Symbolism?"

"No."

"Here." She pulls a paperback from a drawer in her side table. "Take it for a bit. You may want to get your own copy. Some interesting things in there. What I just shared with you is mostly from there."

"Thanks. I will. I really appreciate it. I also want to get one about working with dreams."

"Make sure to be selective. There's a lot of junk out there."

"I will." Kate flips through the book.

"Have you shared your dream with David?"

"No. But I will. I just want to sit with it a little while." Kate pauses, then looks at Marta. "You know, things feel a bit better."

"With David?"

"Yeah. Like there might be hope. But there's still something in me that doesn't trust him."

"And why is that?" asks Marta.

"He might have secrets. And I'm so tired of him saying he'll do something, then not."

"Yes."

"It's hard to have been disappointed for so long." Kate closes her eyes.

"What are you thinking?"

"I feel like I have no idea who I really am."

"From darkness comes birth. It is the womb." Marta's lips slowly curl upward. "I think you do know who you are. You've been a stay-at-home mom since your first birth. That is an awfully long time for a creative person."

"I've been thinking about my jaguar dream. I feel like if I continue to stay in my house, doing only what I've been doing, I could create danger there. There's risk in the unknown—also in staying with what's comfortable."

"Unlived creativity can turn in on a person. Destruction is the polarity of creation." That really resonates. "You've used your creativity with your boys, in your mothering," Marta points out. "It's a beautiful use, by the way. And I think as they grow older, there is something else knocking on your door."

"Like a big black cat?"

"Oh yes." Marta laughs. "Not so subtle, huh?"

"Marta?"

"Yes?"

"How does your life work so well?"

"Who says my life works?"

☽ ● ●

She sits at her desk, pen in hand. What an assumption to presume anyone's life really works. Marta's stark honesty was refreshing. There's something to be said for letting go of what anyone else thinks.

Kate thinks of her childhood. Her mother. Her household in the fellowship. Did all of that have more of an influence on her than she realized? Is her intense longing for intimacy due to those early imprints? And wounds?

She has always been extremely sensitive. She easily could have picked up on her mom's despair. And turmoil.

Her mom had been hurt by her own grandfather. Molested. Then Kate learned that her mom was retraumatized emotionally by one of the senior elders when he blamed her for the sexual abuse she endured as a little girl. She went from being one of the "righteous" fellowship members to one of the "fallen." And as the wife of a junior elder, she was very much under the patriarchal thumb.

Kate was so young then. Only five or six years old. What if that's why she started wetting her bed? It was around the same time.

Has Kate been holding on to patterns passed down from her mom—possibly even generationally—in ways that impact her now?

Why is the main character in the novel she is writing so taken with the male voice?

Realizing her pen has fallen from her grip, Kate picks it up and continues writing.

Jennifer

She does not want to be here but agreed to come. Jennifer leans in toward James. "I need to tell you something."

"James? Can you look at Jennifer?" Lark asks.

He lifts his eyes to meet hers.

"I need to tell you," Jennifer continues, "that if I had known about what you were doing back then, it would have broken my heart."

"I'm so—"

"Please." Jennifer holds up her hand. "Don't say anything."

James is quiet.

"It's too much. I don't know why you even married me." Jennifer takes a deep breath. She must say the words. "I want a divorce."

James's head falls heavy. His entire being seems to deflate.

"Are you sure about this?" Lark asks. "Even if James is willing to do the work and make some changes?"

"I lived those years, my youth, with a man who's slept with other women since we were dating. While I was home having and taking care of his babies! I'm sure."

Lark steps in. "James, can you hear how angry Jennifer is?"

He nods, eyes still on the floor.

"And are you angry at Jennifer's betrayal as well?"

Again, he nods.

"And how do you feel about the idea of divorcing?"

James says nothing.

"Jennifer?" Lark changes her focus. "Are you planning to act on this right away, or can you give it some time?"

"I can't do this anymore. I know we'll always be a family. I hope we can be friends someday. But I'm already out of this marriage. An affair is one thing—it can be a symptom of a problem, but multiple one-night stands? I have no idea who all those women were James slept with. That's not what—who—I want to be married to. I don't care how long ago it was. It happened." Jennifer turns to face James. "You did that."

They are both weeping now. Even Lark has tears in her eyes. She places a box of tissues within reach. Jennifer feels the walls closing in. She wipes her nose and lifts her head. "I don't want to talk anymore. I'm filing this week." She grabs her things, only partially seeing.

"I'm here, Jennifer," Lark offers, "if you want to call."

Jennifer pulls the door open, steps out, and lets it shut behind her. She turns immediately down the hall, toward the ladies' room. Pulling open a stall, she collapses. Jennifer tears off wads of toilet paper. She sprays endlessly from her eyes and nose, the reality of her words reaching into every corner of her. Sorrow filling her.

Her lonely childhood. Her deep longing to be seen—really seen. Loved. And her children. How will it be for Chloe and Jimmy? She is responsible for breaking up their home. Or at least responsible for not covering up that it's already broken.

The drive is long. She has two Cokes from the little Thai place. Jennifer drinks them greedily, the sweetness soaking into her very being. There is somehow a calm at the core of her. It will be hard. Probably unbearable. Yet she slowly begins to feel herself moving into the eye of the storm.

☽ ● ●

CHLOE SMELLS LIKE STRAWBERRIES. JENNIFER BREATHES IN THE smell of her freshly shampooed hair. "How about I put Jimmy to bed, and you and I sneak into my room for some time together?"

"Okay!" Chloe cracks a smile. "Can we have hot chocolate?"

"Yes."

"And maybe popcorn?" Her eyes bright.

"Yes."

"And—"

"Don't push it, kid," Jennifer shoots her daughter a fake-stern look as her lips betray her teasing.

Chloe laughs. "Come get me when he's asleep."

"You got it. Read a little."

"And, Mom?" Chloe seems calm.

"Yeah?"

"I love my new comforter and lamp."

Jennifer kisses her forehead and watches her daughter skip to her bedroom. Should she tell her tonight?

"Jimmy, need any help?" Jennifer yells.

"No."

"You brush your teeth?"

"No."

"Come on, buddy. Let's get going." She peers into her son's bedroom to find him sitting on his floor naked, except for a pirate hat, playing LEGOs. She suppresses a laugh.

"What are you doing?"

"Making a pirate ship."

"Wow. That's great, sweetie. Save the rest for tomorrow and come get your jammies on."

"I don't want to," he says.

"I'll read you a quick something. How about your favorite funny poem?"

"Yes!"

"Let me help you get dressed, and I'll get the book while you brush your teeth. Did you go to the bathroom?"

"No."

"Then do that too." She slides the pajama top over Jimmy's head. Then he steps into the bottoms.

"I know," he answers.

Jimmy bolts toward the bathroom while Jennifer looks on his white bookshelf. She finds the book and climbs under the covers with it, scooting to one side. The toilet flushes. Jimmy bounds into the room and onto the bed.

"Batman tackle!" He jumps, full weight, onto Jennifer. She wraps her arms around him, kissing him.

"I'll suck the life out of you, Batman!" she threatens. She pulls his neck to her lips and blows on his skin. He shrieks with delight. "Okay, sweetie, come on in." She rolls him off her, pulls the blankets out from under his little body, then over him and up to his chin. His comforter has that brand-new smell.

Jimmy loves her funny voices and does them along with her. How comforting the familiar is. How sweet, the tucking in. Jennifer closes the book and carefully rises from his bed. "Good night, sweetie."

"One more?" Jimmy asks, just in case.

"Not tonight. We'll do two tomorrow night."

"Mama?"

"Yeah?"

"I love my doggie." Jimmy squeezes his new stuffed dog.

"I'm so glad. I hoped you would. Night, sweet thing." Her daughter is waiting.

Can Jennifer hold herself together? Opening the pantry door, she grabs a popcorn packet and rips off the plastic. She puts it in the microwave and opens the refrigerator, looking for milk. She finds a half gallon almost full and takes chocolate syrup from the door. Jennifer pours milk into a saucepan and turns the burner to medium. She stirs it, turning around as the microwave beeps four times.

"Ready?" asks Chloe. Jennifer looks to see her daughter wearing her favorite pink nightgown. Rosy cheeked and waiting.

"Almost. Can you get the big blue bowl out of that cupboard? The popcorn's done."

"Jimmy's sleeping." Chloe searches for the bowl.

"Oh, good."

"I peeked, and he was snoring."

"Loud?"

"Yeah. Can I put the chocolate in?"

"Sure. Hand me that bowl, and you can put it right in with the milk." They create their bedtime snack together. "Let's put it on a tray to bring into my room," Jennifer offers. That way they can sit close. "For special girl time."

"Yay!"

They bring everything in and get comfortable in bed.

"Yummy!" Chloe grins.

"Tell me about it. I forgot how good this tastes. Like cozy in the mouth."

"Like a warm blanket wrapped all around your tongue."

They laugh.

"Chloe, I know I've been really busy lately. I'm glad to have time with you."

"Me too." They sip their hot chocolate. "Mom?"

"Yeah?"

"How come you painted your room red?"

Passion. Scarlet. Bold. "I've always wanted a deep red bedroom," she answers. It feels womb-like. And her new gold comforter is luxurious. Jennifer worked hard to put her room together. It's exactly how she'd envisioned it.

"Mom?"

"Yeah, sweetness?"

"Do you hate Daddy?"

Jennifer's stomach lurches. "Does it seem like I do?"

"I don't know." Chloe shrugs. "Just that you might."

"Hmm. I think this is one of those things that's difficult to understand. It's complicated."

"Like how?"

"Like I still care about him. And want to be his friend. And it works better for us to live in different places."

"Forever?" Chloe's eyes widen.

"Possibly, sweet girl. We're talking about it."

"Are you . . . getting a divorce?"

Jennifer tastes bile in the back of her throat. She takes a sip of her chocolate, now more warm than hot.

"We're trying to figure that out. But I'll tell you, either way, we will always care about each other and always, always love and care for you and Jimmy. Always. No matter what." She is fighting tears. Wanting to be truthful—and careful. Chloe . . . "Do you know that?" She touches her daughter's soft hand.

"I guess. I just liked it better. How it was."

"I know. I really do."

Chloe leans over and rests her head on Jennifer's chest. Then her body lets go, releasing huge sobs. She lies on Jennifer's heart, wrapped in her arms. Jennifer strokes Chloe's hair, laying her cheek on the top of her head. Jennifer cries with her.

"I love you so much, sweetheart."

Jennifer reaches and pulls a box of tissues onto the bed. The mugs have not spilled. She lifts and places them on her side table. Jennifer hands Chloe a tissue and brings another to her nose.

"Oh, sweetie . . ."

Chloe blows her nose as her breathing calms. Jennifer holds her close.

"It's okay to be sad. Or mad," she tells her. "It's not fair this is happening. And I am so, so sorry."

Chloe begins to cry again. This time, soft whimpers. Jennifer's eyes well up. Is it possible to ever run out of tears?

"Can I sleep in your bed?" Chloe's voice is faint.

"Yes, sweet one." They squeeze each other tight, staying like that for a long time.

"I"—Chloe giggles—"have to pee!"

"Me too!"

As Chloe gets up and walks to the bathroom, Jennifer takes hold of the mugs of now-cold, brown liquid. She places them on the tray along with the half-eaten bowl of popcorn and carries them to the kitchen. Jennifer shudders to think of the pain she is creating for her young daughter.

Yet Chloe is not her. Chloe is not alone. She has a good mother. Brother. And father. Jennifer had none of that growing up.

Kate

A precious phone conversation with Rachel. Why is it so hard to find the time? "Don't you remember in college that class I took junior year, about the animal aspect?"

"No." Kate doesn't remember it at all.

"You don't? How some cultures believe everyone has an animal counterpart?"

Kate tries to jog her memory. "I honestly don't . . ."

"You came to visit that semester, and we took turns with, like, five people, walking and figuring out what animals we were. Remember who we said you were?"

"No."

"Jaguar!"

Goose bumps pop up all over Kate's body.

"Oh, Rachel. That just gave me chills. Really?"

"I can't believe you don't remember."

"I'm so glad I called you. That's wild!"

"That's you."

Kate is quiet.

"You there?" asks Rachel.

"Yeah."

"You always used to say, 'What you see is what you get,' about yourself. I never knew why you said that."

"I thought it was true."

"I remember the day I realized you believed it. I never did."

Kate can sense Rachel shaking her head. "You didn't?"

"I always knew there was more to you than that."

"Really?"

"Yes. Kate, I grew up watching you. When you'd get ready for school or to go on a date. Everything."

Kate smiles. "I miss you."

"I miss you too. You should visit."

"I'm actually signed up to go to a workshop out west fairly soon, but I'll need to come right home."

"What's the workshop about?"

"It's with the man who wrote that book about dreaming I told you about," Kate shares excitedly. "This teacher is all about empowering the dreamer. Some shamanism too."

"I totally want to hear about it."

"I'm nervous," Kate confesses.

"Oh, it'll be great!"

Kate flinches. "Especially leaving the boys."

"How long is it?"

"Five days."

"You'll be fine. Really. It'll be good for them. And David. About time too! Wait, hold on a sec." Rachel yells something. "Kate, I gotta go. I'm so sorry. We're going to a party, and we're late."

"Rachel?"

"Yeah?"

"I love you."

"I love you too. And I think it's awesome what you're doing."

Kate's heart swells. "Thank you so much. Have fun at the party."

"I will," says Rachel. "Let's talk soon."

"Okay, bye."

"Bye!"

Kate puts down the phone, remembering the dream she had during Rachel's last visit. It was powerful.

She lay on her back in the middle of a circle of stones. People stood just outside the stones, surrounding her. The leader was shooting something through the bottom of her feet. It was electric. Her legs vibrated as the energy shot through her entire body. They were shaking violently—so was the bed.

Rachel was sleeping next to her. David was out of town. Kate suddenly felt panicked about frightening her, even while still in the dream. For a moment, Kate was in both places at once, like with the flying dream. Then she came back to her physical body. Her bed. She turned immediately to look at Rachel. Still asleep. What a relief. Kate's legs slowly grew still, although they continued to buzz for a long time.

How could a dream literally make her legs shake like that?

She feels a sudden chill, her skin craving the comfort of a warm bath. Moving to the bathroom, she runs water in the tub. A candle would be good. Vanilla scented. As she reaches for the candle on the table by the window, Kate catches a glimpse of herself in the mirror.

How had she not noticed the change? Her hair hangs longer than ever, halfway down her back. And the grays are starting to show. Not too much, but they're there. Her face looks longer. Leaner. Older. She smiles at her reflection. Hopefully wiser. Her image smiles back. Green eyes.

Green eyes? When did that happen?

Kate moves close to the mirror. There is brown right around her pupils, and that's it. All the rest is green. Not even hazel. Green. Almost blue toward the edge.

Kate shakes her head in disbelief and feels another chill.

The water. Kate turns off the faucet and walks back to the mirror. There they are—green. Her eyes were so dark when she was little, she couldn't even see her pupils.

Kate undresses and eases herself into the tub, her flesh prickling with the thrill of the heat. She takes in a deep breath, filling her ribs, expanding them sideways. Like she practiced during her last massage.

And now she's going to a workshop. On the other side of the country. With a dreamworker. Kate thinks about the book she just finished. It was fascinating and lit a fire in her. It said a person can set the intention to be given a dream and to remember it that night. Maybe she'll try it.

☽ ● ●

"It was a kind of dream within a dream, with the end so vivid." Kate has become increasingly comfortable sharing her dreams with Marta. She feels there is no safer place.

"You were given a job to do?" asks Marta. "Or something like that?"

"I had undergone a series of tasks. Tests, actually." Kate closes her eyes, settling back into the memory of the dream. "There's a small audience, or group of witnesses, watching. Before my final and most challenging task, the woman in charge tells me I might feel the need at some point to take off all my clothes." Kate laughs. "I tell her I won't. And then it begins.

"It's hazy, whatever is happening. I feel how hard I'm working but am not sure what I'm actually doing. There's a growing intensity, like I'm working myself into an increasingly frenzied state. Then I am dancing—with every fiber of my being. It's building . . .

"The heat begins to take hold.

"Suddenly, I'm completely overwhelmed with the need to take off all my clothes, and I do. I tear off every single piece—my dance heightening. I'm fully aware I am naked and I don't care. I can't stop. I don't want to.

"I dance and dance and dance . . . coming to the full height of my power . . . climaxing to a place beyond myself . . . as *I become fire itself!*

"Then it is over. The woman in charge wraps me in a blanket and we sit. I am completely spent. Nothing left. The woman looks into me and asks me what I have learned.

"I tell her, 'I have seen the depth of my own sadness.'"

Marta's eyes are kind. Like the woman with the blanket.

"When I woke up, I had the unshakable feeling it was real."

"Do you know what you were doing in the first tasks?" Marta asks.

"No. But I felt them. They were progressively more difficult." Something suddenly comes to mind. "I just remembered something. Two things. Do you have any paper?"

Marta hands her a piece of paper from her notepad. Kate takes a pen from her purse and writes. She takes a moment to read it to herself, then shares her words with Marta.

"Until I am able to bear the weight of my own sadness, I will continue to project it into the world," she reads aloud. "And one more thing. About the dream. I was told I passed the test."

A pause. Kate wonders aloud, "Why was I being tested?"

"Who knows. Perhaps you'll know over time. You're doing good work and taking worthwhile risks. Moving through a lot. I'm glad you're able to share your dreams with me." Marta smiles. Then she squints in mock seriousness. "Now, I have one small request."

Kate raises her eyebrows.

"Have some fun, have a good laugh." Marta's eyes are playful. They seem to sparkle. "Maybe see a funny movie. Have David take you out for a nice dinner."

Kate laughs at herself. "I know, it's all about balance. That's what Nia and I say."

"And keep writing what you are living. It may be important for others to read one day, other women. To see the way you have dealt with your life."

Suddenly, Marta looks otherworldly. She appears taller than normal. Kate is mesmerized. Goose bumps ripple down her spine. She becomes aware of her own body. Of the couch beneath her. She shakes her hands, releasing the intensity down her arms and out through her fingers. She turns to look at the clock. It's the end of the session.

As Marta opens the door to show Kate out, she says, "I believe if you and David can continue to work through things and learn to really live in truth with one another, you will be exceptional—both of you."

Kate steps out into the sunlight, immediately blinded. There are moments where she gets it. She sees it all and feels so awake. Then she is struck blind. Asleep again. Struggling to find her bearings.

Jennifer

JENNIFER HANGS HER LAST PICTURE. STANDING BACK, HAMMER IN hand, she takes in the room. What a change. Only now is she beginning to know and feel herself. No more adapting and accommodating at the expense of herself. The phone rings, startling her.

"Hello?"

"Jennifer?" She stiffens. James. "I need to talk to you."

"Why?" she asks.

"I need to know"—his voice cracks—"if this is what you really want."

"You know what, James? It took me a long time to come to this. Is it what I want? No. But it's where I am."

"If you don't want it, how can you file for divorce? This week? Give it six months or something. Then see how you feel. I haven't been with anyone else in a long time. You know that. I live for this family."

"You actually think I know it because you say it. But your words mean nothing to me."

"I know in the past—"

"No. Now. Always. You say you're here now, but you're not. Not really."

"But I'm trying."

"You hurt me at a time in my life when I was completely open to you. And young. You missed it all. Me. The kids. And now you think you just get to have us. Like we should sit around waiting until you're done sleeping with all the women you want, then everything's fine because you say you're sorry?" Hot rage. She can't stop. "You don't get to have me now!" Jennifer tries to steady herself. "I'm not even here anymore. Not for you. If I stayed with you, it would be a lie. And don't think I haven't thought this through from every angle."

"I don't think you have," James grasps. "What about Jimmy and Chloe? You want them to think this is what happens? That things can't be worked out? Their mom and dad don't love each other? They have to split their time for the rest of their lives between their parents? Is that fair to them?"

Jennifer forces herself to take deep breaths, then answers. "Is it fair to them to put their mother at risk while she's nursing them, possibly—probably—even pregnant?"

"And their mother, having an affair while they're in school?"

"It wasn't going to happen any other way, James. You never would've told me if I hadn't told you first. Charlotte. And those women you slept with—that you didn't even know. At least the affair I can understand. You saw something in her. Cared about her."

"I always felt Charlotte was the real betrayal. The others, I didn't plan, they just happened. I was dumb. And drunk. Every time. With Charlotte too. There was a time I thought I loved her and was going to leave you." He breaks into sobs. "But I didn't . . ."

"Maybe you should have. You probably deserve each other."

"Jennifer, that's . . ."

She waits silently as he cries. Her floor needs sweeping. Dirty laundry overflows the hamper.

James speaks through his tears. "I never loved her. I thought I did. I couldn't breathe. I had no right getting married when I did. I didn't know what I was doing. I was acting out."

"I hear you. And do you realize at that same time you say you had no business being married, you *were* married. To *me*. You kept me right where you wanted. In a perfect cage. Until you were ready. And now you think you are, but guess what? I'm not. I grew up. I'm not so young anymore and not nearly so stupid."

"I love you," he gasps. "I didn't . . . I promise that was all a long time ago. It wasn't even me."

"It *was* you! That's what you don't get. Own it! You are the same person who did those things. And so am I! When I had my affair! I did that! Me! At least I can be real about it."

James meets her anger. "But I wasn't! I don't feel the same! That was me acting out my wounds from childhood. Needing to act like a little boy. Rebelling. I was acting from an unconscious place."

Jennifer feels heat everywhere. "You have no idea, James. I'm not leaving because I'm angry. And I know I've hurt you. I was set up to betray you. Conscious or not, you opened the door I'm walking out of when you chose your lies over loving me—" She can no longer resist the tears. "And our babies. You didn't choose me. James. You didn't. You took me and put me where you wanted. Because you probably really did want to be married. But *I'm* a person too. What makes you think your experience was more important than mine? You didn't have the right."

"I am so sorry." James's words are genuine. "How many times can I say it?"

Jennifer is suddenly calm. "It doesn't matter. That's what I realize now. The trust is gone. It doesn't matter how many times you say it. I don't feel it. I don't want it."

There is a long silence.

"Can we talk with Lark? One more time?" he pleads.

Jennifer releases a huge breath she hadn't realized she was holding. "No. Not together."

"So, this is it? This is how it ends? Just like this?"

"I guess."

"Well, Lark said if this is what you really want, there's nothing I can do."

"It's what's happening," says Jennifer. "What I wanted was very different."

There is a long silence.

Finally, Jennifer speaks. "I gotta go. I have . . . I need to hang up."

"Okay."

"Good-bye, James."

Jennifer collapses onto her bed, phone still in hand. She begins to feel pulled under. Carefully, she holds up the phone and dials.

"Hello?"

Jennifer is unable to find her voice.

"Hello?"

"I-I'm really sorry," Jennifer lets out a gasp. "Can you come over? I'm—"

"Jen? Jen, I can come. I'll be there in ten minutes."

"Thank you."

"Just hold on. I'll be right there."

"Thank you, Betty."

"I'm on my way."

Kate

What a good class today. She actually took the risk of writing and sharing a dream aloud with the group. A big one too. Thank goodness she didn't cry, although it would have been fine if she had.

Kate finishes her banana and decides to go for a walk. She needs to move after sitting so long. She allows her attention to rest within her body. She still feels it. The heartbreak. She had the dream three days ago, yet it was haunting. The leftover despair in her heart feels heavy.

As she walks, Kate allows the depth of her pain to fill her. In the dream, she had somehow fallen into her worst nightmare and was living with the loss of her family—her beloved boys. How would she ever live through such a loss? Unbearable.

In the dream, she was completely and existentially alone. That was at the heart of her suffering. And it was magnified by the fact that she remembered what she had lost. She wouldn't—couldn't—let go.

Kate's mind begins to rearrange her thoughts in an unusual way. Everything seems to turn upside down. Then her heart opens. Tears well up. Sorrow erupts, working its way out from where it has settled. Moving up from her heart, toward her throat.

Kate ignores the impulse to swallow. A strange sound escapes her. Suddenly, it rises completely. In one abrupt motion, it flies out through the top of her head. Free.

When she returns home, David is there.

"Hey," Kate greets him. "I want to tell you something. It's a dream I had, a few days ago. A big one. About you and the boys."

David listens intently to the whole thing. He doesn't say a word. When Kate is done, her head drops.

"Come here," he says. David wraps his arms around Kate. He holds her tight. Then he pulls back and looks at her. Really looks.

"Your eyes . . . they're green."

"I saw that myself just the other day . . ."

They hold each other.

"David, there was a time when things felt so bad, I wished I never met you. But—" Kate can hardly get the words out, "Peter and Ben . . ." She spent years wishing things were different from how they were. "I don't feel that now."

David holds her face in his hands. His gaze is gentle. Loving. He leans in and kisses her. The kiss is passionate. Surprising. Kate feels her body grow warm, spreading from her middle, moving down between her legs and up into her heart.

David pulls her even closer. He moves his hands over her breasts, down her body, to her lower back. Like he used to. Kate begins to burn with heat.

"I want you," he whispers, his voice low. He unbuttons her blouse. It's already halfway off. His movements are focused. "I want you," he repeats. His breath, hot. He licks her neck. Ears.

"Oh my God."

Kate is melting. She breathes him in. Deep want. He touches between her legs. She moans. He continues . . .

"Take me," she whispers. "Please. Take me."

David tears off her pants, underwear too. And unzips his own. He presses her to the wall. What is this? They are still in the kitchen. David picks her up. He looks into her eyes. She feels herself surrender.

"You are . . ." He doesn't finish. David's breath deepens.

Kate wraps her legs around him. David thrusts himself into her. As he does, a loud moan escapes her. Then all thought disappears. Their energy continues to build . . . David and Kate move as one . . . the intensity growing . . . growing . . . Coming finally to climax. Simultaneously. Something deep within Kate opens. Hot liquid pours out of her.

"What was that?" David gasps.

Kate erupts into stunned laughter. "I don't know!"

"My God!"

They continue to laugh, falling to the floor.

"That was . . ."

"Hot!" Kate smiles. "Amazing. You're amazing."

"You are . . . so beautiful." He gently touches her cheek. "We're soaking wet! What the hell happened? Did you pee?"

"No! That's not even possible."

"Did you just . . . ejaculate?" he asks.

"I don't know!"

They can't stop laughing.

"That can happen for women, you know." David smiles. "It's rare."

"This. Whatever this is. Is rare."

☽ ● ●

Kate is embarrassed. And excited. She can share anything with Marta.

"And what happened," Marta asks, "after you and David made love?"

"We had takeout with Ben and Peter." Kate still feels herself blushing. "Then after they went to bed, David and I watched a movie together. Close. Sitting together on the couch."

"Ohh," Marta coos.

"Oh!" Kate remembers, "And I had a dream that night. My arms grew clear up to the sky and my legs down into the earth. I was so big that our whole home could fit inside my trunk. I was an enormous tree!"

"Wow, Kate, it sounds as if a lot is happening. Your roots are deepening, in many ways."

"I didn't know you could have that kind of sex with someone you've been with for so long."

"Relationship is an interesting thing," Marta muses. "It sometimes opens and closes."

"David thinks I ejaculated."

"Sounds like it. Has that ever happened?"

"No." Kate can't help giggling.

"How did you feel?"

"Like I was cracked wide open." Kate thinks for a moment. "And safe."

"I wonder if this emotional opening, and deepening, that's starting to happen with you and David may be . . ." Marta stops, searching for the right words.

Kate feels calm and patient.

"It's quite admirable. Many couples go their separate ways when they feel that disconnect. There are many ebbs and flows in marriage."

"I'm getting that."

"You keep hanging in there," Marta encourages. "You will continue to grow, not unlike that tree. You have your workshop coming up, right?"

"I do. I'm nervous."

"Your boys will be fine. You will be fine."

"I don't like going on airplanes." Kate's stomach turns over. "I always think if I die, Peter and Ben would be without a mother."

"It is really something to be a mother." Marta's smile is reassuring. "I had a friend who told me it's as if once you have children, you forever wear your heart on the outside of your body."

"That's it exactly."

"And in the moment where you feel that vulnerability, just imagine your boys with all the protection they need around them. Yourself too. That is important in life and with the work you're starting to do."

"I feel that. And I feel the black jaguar with me more and more."

"I see her in you," says Marta.

Kate's face suddenly feels hot. "You do?"

Marta smiles and nods.

"What does she look like?"

Marta looks at Kate. She is quiet for a long time.

"What?"

"You seem more grounded."

"I feel more grounded."

"And something else . . . I can't quite put my finger on it. I'm not sure what it is."

Something catches Kate's attention. The light dancing on the wall.

"Ahh, that's it." Marta scoots to the edge of her chair. "You seem . . . content."

Kate smiles big.

"You know," says Marta, "I thought of you the other day."

"How?"

"I was at the beach, renting a cabin for a brief getaway. And I went down to the water right before sunset. It was a beautiful sky." Oranges. Pinks. Deep momentary reds. "I noticed to my left a woman, blond hair, nice looking, sitting on a blanket. She had a glass of wine and a bottle next to her. I don't know if she was waiting for someone to join her. She sat with a notebook, watching the sunset."

Kate imagines the woman Marta is describing sipping her wine, taking in the beautiful colors as they peak. Enjoying her solitude.

"Then I look on my right. A family sits, not far away. Actually, the man and woman were sitting on the blanket, their two children playing at the water. It was cold, and they screamed as it came over their ankles."

Kate sees Ben and Peter in her mind's eye.

"The woman there looked like you, or something about her. I could see her fingers touching the man's, just barely, but clearly they were connected." Marta pauses. "Yet also they were in their own experience. The two of them, as they watched their children play."

A tear runs down Kate's cheek.

"Ohh," Marta coos again tenderly. "You are doing good work, Kate. One can spend a lifetime doing this work."

"Thank you, Marta." Kate nods. "Thank you so much."

☽ ● ●

Holding the feeling of contentment all day, Kate feels soft and full. As she tucks Ben into bed, she holds him tight.

"Know what, Mommy?" Ben asks.

"What, love?"

"You can see the future in your dreams."

"How so?"

"Last night, I dreamed I was at school and Miss Fain gave us a math test. I saw the whole thing." Ben plays with Kate's hair, twirling it around his fingers. "Then today, at school, she did. And it was the exact same. I knew all the answers from when I did it in my dream. It was really easy." Ben. A dreamer too.

"You," Kate says, "are astonishing. I love that you just told me that."

"It's really true."

"I believe you. I really and truly do." She hugs him. "That is so cool. I love you, Ben."

"Love you, Mommy."

As she turns out the light, quietly closing his door, Kate thinks of how much Ben reminds her of herself when she was little. He looks so much like her. And he's always had a familiar energy. How lucky to have two boys, each so different, each so exactly who he is. She walks into the kitchen. David stands at the counter, opening a bottle of wine.

"Red?" he asks. "Sound good?"

"Sounds great."

Kate takes the good wineglasses from the top shelf and holds them out. David pours and hands one to Kate. He raises his glass. "To you."

Kate meets his glass with her own. "And you."

The sound rings through the air.

Jennifer

Jennifer sits in the warmth of the sunlight. She silently reads over her words.

Dear James,

I don't even think I realized the truth of my own words until I spoke them. I'm not angry anymore. I still feel sadness—at the loss of a dream—but then, the dream never was a reality, was it? Maybe we've gone through the level of drama we have so we could have the opportunity to see, really see, ourselves.

Can we choose to find the gift in all of this? I don't want to become bitter in the years to come. I do not want this experience to define me. I will continue to work through my feelings about your betrayals, and my own, for some time, I am sure. Yet there must be a way to remain open. That is my hope, anyway. I see the decision to divorce as holding a level of integrity and truth. I do not hate you, nor will I ever be separate from you. We share these two beautiful children; children we will continue to love, nurture, and protect.

Can we offer them a safe haven from our painful past and present complexity of feelings about one another? Can we give them this gift? I am trying to find a way to honor myself, Chloe, Jimmy, and also you. I hear the level of devastation you feel about my decision, and for that, I am truly sorry.

This is the way for me. I am no longer with you. Too much has taken place, and I'm choosing to stay with the part of myself that can no longer participate in a marriage with you.

We will always be in a relationship with one another, through our children. And I want very much for that to be supportive and positive. I promise you I will not speak negatively of you. I will not harm you or Jimmy and Chloe by acting out the hurt I've incurred in that way. I will lift you up in their eyes by responding to the many wonderful qualities you have and are able to bring to their lives.

I give you this letter as an offering of peace. I will honor whatever decision you make in how you relate to me. Yet I ask, from the bottom of my heart, that you put our children first. They are our babies. We decided to have them in love, and they need to experience that love, in and through us.

With genuine hope,
Jennifer

This is her truth. She must send it now. Before she changes her mind. She addresses the envelope to her old house, places a stamp in the corner, folds the letter, and seals it.

It's a mile or so to the nearest mailbox. She will walk with her own two feet to take it there. James will get it tomorrow. He will read it. And what will he do? Her children's future depends on his response. This now-divorced family's quality of life depends on him. She has made her choice. Finally.

The sun feels good, piercing through her almost porcelain skin. The ground beneath her is solid as she walks. Jennifer reaches the blue mailbox, opens it, and watches the letter fall. Relief. It is done. She has handed James her most loving self. She can only hope to receive the same. Even if it takes time.

Jennifer's stomach growls. She realizes she hasn't eaten yet and decides to continue into town. She is glad she brought her backpack. The walk is soothing.

By the time she reaches the hole-in-the-wall Mexican place, she's ravenous. Jennifer orders her favorite breakfast burrito. And a large coffee. They make it with cinnamon. She sips the hot liquid, taking in the aroma. When her burrito is ready, she eats hungrily. She could eat two.

So much has happened. She thought she might never come through it. Is this the other side? Or at least the beginning of it?

Jennifer steps out into the bright sunlight, finally full, coffee in hand. She blinks. Her mind must be playing tricks on her. But—no. The last time she saw him, he was walking away. She had nothing in her to stop him. Andrew stands in front of her. Sun cascades all around him.

"How are you?" he asks.

"Okay. You?"

"I've been better."

"You look good," she offers.

"So do you." Andrew's eyes are intense. "As always."

She laughs.

"I've been seeing someone else. Just twice."

"I'm happy for you." She's surprised she really is happy.

"She's nothing like you."

"That's good." They share a laugh.

"Jennifer. She doesn't hold a candle to you." She turns away. "I really do think I'm the man for you. I love you the way you need to be loved."

Anguish is all she remembers. "Thank you," she says, looking right at him. "I mean it. I feel like I was dying back then."

"Can I call you? Can I walk you home?" Andrew moves closer.

She feels his heat. She steps back.

"Jennifer."

"I have some sorting out to do."

"One kiss?"

She shakes her head, tears suddenly welling up. "Goodbye, Andrew." She walks away. Raw. Relieved. Suddenly, Jennifer begins to laugh and cry at the same time. The movement sweeps through her, head to toe.

As she enters her apartment, the colors seem brighter than usual. Jennifer falls heavily onto the couch. Sleep comes . . .

She wakes up disoriented, thinking of a woman. Exotic. With almond eyes. Did she dream her? Jennifer looks at her watch. She reaches for her purse and heads out the door. The dream stays with her as she drives, overriding her hurry.

YEAR FOUR

BECOMING

Kate

Nia looks adorable wearing the mismatched, only-clean clothes she has left. "You're not going to bring it up, are you?" she asks.

"What?"

"The workshop . . ."

Kate folds Ben's favorite shirt and lays it on top of a clean pile. She remembers buying that shirt. She watches as Nia opens the laundry room door, happy to help with her broken washer situation. It's good to have her over. But what to say?

"Thanks again. You're a lifesaver!" Nia calls. From the sound of it, her head is halfway in the dryer.

"Don't fall in!"

"Don't worry!" Nia laughs. "I can't find . . . Oh, here it is." She reemerges holding her favorite bra. "Why don't you want to talk about it?"

"I . . . I don't know."

"Hey, it's me. What are you worried about?"

"There's weird and there's weird." Kate takes a breath. "And this is *weird*."

"I can handle it." Nia points to a sweatshirt just beyond reach. "Will you toss me that?"

Kate does.

"It's been a long time since we did laundry together." Nia smiles.

"First time I've done it without having to make a therapy appointment midway."

Nia shakes her head with a half smile. She is well aware of Kate's laundry issues.

"Kate." Nia's voice is gentle. "I'm here for you."

"I know, I'm sorry. I just . . . feel like I'm not completely back yet. Or something."

"Was it a good experience, at least?"

"Yeah. It really was, once I got into it. I spent the first two days wondering what the hell I was doing there."

"Did you feel good about the dream teacher?"

"You know"—Kate looks up—"I did."

"How many participants were there?"

"Only ten."

"Nice."

"It was. I expected more. I guess usually there are. You know how wary I am about groups."

"Yes . . ."

"There's always *one*." Kate makes a face.

"Often more than one," Nia agrees.

"Uh-huh. But there wasn't." Kate nods, nearing the bottom of the pile. She should do laundry with Nia more often. "I felt like I could be me. Actually"—she can share this with Nia—"it was more than that. I felt like during the week, I stepped into myself. If that makes sense."

"Yes, it does."

"It had to do with the group. How they witnessed who I was."

"You felt seen."

Why had she been worried about sharing with Nia? What an unusual week away. She felt more herself and further from her everyday self. Like with the bus. "I feel freer than I ever have. And intensely private."

"I respect that. Will you please just tell me what happened with the jaguar? You said something intriguing to me on the phone about it, then I won't ask anymore."

"Only if we go down and make coffee." Kate could really use a cup. "We can come back for the next load."

"Deal."

"That wasn't even painful!" Kate looks at the piles of clean, folded clothes.

Nia offers her hands and pulls Kate up. They move downstairs, where Kate washes out the coffeepot. With beans ground and water prepared, Kate turns on the coffeemaker.

"Do you have any chocolate?"

"I have good chocolate." Kate opens the cupboard, pulling out a bar. "Catch!"

"How appropriate!" Nia stares into the yellow eyes of a black jaguar. "Eighty-eight percent cacao. And you have to tell me now. With these eyes staring at me?"

"Okay, but you can't share this with anyone. It feels . . . almost sacred."

"My word." Nia places her hand on her heart.

How to start? "So, the teacher starts drumming. That's the way to create a kind of bridge between worlds. What he calls ordinary and non-ordinary reality. Here and there. Some shamans take peyote, but a drum or rattle serves the same purpose, with a rhythmic, monotone beat."

Kate pounds her hand steadily on the counter for a few beats. "It's the third day and I go right into it, a kind of altered state. I'm lying on my back. My bandanna over my eyes, so it's dark. And I'm holding my moonstone, by the way."

"You took it?"

Kate nods. "And guess who came to greet me, in the journey?"

Nia glances down at the chocolate bar wrapper.

Kate nods again. "And you can open that, by the way. It will enhance the story."

Nia opens the wrapper and breaks off a piece, placing a chocolate square on her tongue. She closes her eyes, gesturing for Kate to go on.

"She tells me to follow her . . . and I do."

The coffeemaker beeps three times. Nia's expression says it can wait.

"Then the black jaguar suddenly turns on me. Goes right for my throat. She shakes me . . . until I die. I begin to leave my body. It's so real. And I'm also fully aware I'm lying on the floor in the middle of my workshop. Both are true. Just in different places, different realities."

"Go on . . ."

"So, I leave my body. I'm going up, up—way up. There's a light that gets brighter and brighter. It begins to encompass me, in layers. It's absolute bliss. Then—" Kate's voice breaks. "I look down. The same black jaguar that killed me is sitting next to my body. Protecting it."

Nia gently touches Kate's arm.

"It was so moving." Kate says through her tears. "Her being my protector."

Nia wraps her arms around Kate.

"Afterward, I couldn't stop crying. It was so powerful."

Nia pulls back enough to look at her. Kate grabs Nia's hand.

"It was a dismemberment. I didn't know. My teacher said it was a traditional shamanic initiation. I feel completely humbled. Please don't tell anyone."

"I would never say a word, Kate. This is yours."

"I know. I just had to say it again. It feels so raw. I'm still processing everything."

"Thank you for telling me," Nia says in earnest. "You can trust me with this. Whatever it means, I think it's fascinating."

"It feels really big."

"Absolutely."

There is a moment of quiet intimacy as Kate and Nia allow the story to settle.

Then Kate smiles. "Coffee?"

"Let me get it." As Nia hands Kate a hot mug, she softly says, "I'm proud of you."

"Thank you. I'm so glad I went. And I'm happy to be back." She sips her coffee. It feels grounding. Kate takes in a nice, deep breath. As she exhales, she feels the immediacy of her surroundings. "Are you and Joseph still up for Friday?"

"We sure are." Nia smiles, sipping her coffee. "I'm looking forward to it."

"It'll be fun."

"It will." Nia looks up. "Do you hear that?" she asks.

"What?"

"Shhh. Listen."

Silence.

"I don't hear anything," says Kate.

"Exactly. The dryer is done."

"No—" Kate mock groans.

"Come on, my brave friend. Back to . . . what did he call it? Ordinary reality!" Kate and Nia burst out laughing.

● ● ●

"Whatcha reading, spiritual stuff?"

Kate looks up to see Ben trying to catch a glimpse of her book cover. "Maybe," she answers.

Peter pipes in from the other room. "Figures!"

Ben laughs gleefully. "You're always doing spiritual stuff."

"It's true!" yells Peter.

Kate hadn't realized. She probably has been, especially since the workshop. She doesn't talk with Peter and Ben about her forming beliefs. Not because she doesn't want to share but because they pay more attention to what she does than says. So, they've noticed a change.

"And writing spiritual stuff—that you never let me read!" Peter adds, still in the other room.

Kate imagines Peter reading her writing. "Not because I'm mean," she says. "It's not appropriate—and not necessarily spiritual, by the way."

"What's it rated?" Peter rates everything, not just movies.

"Where are you, anyway?"

"Library couch."

"R," Kate answers.

"For sexual content?" Peter's interest is piqued. He's recently begun writing himself and seems a natural.

"Some." Kate smiles to herself. "And mature issues. The whole nature of it, hon."

"When will you let me?" he pushes. "When I'm eighteen?"

Kate can't imagine ever wanting him to read it. "I'm not even done yet." Ben has been standing next to her. He slowly sinks into her lap. Kate lays her book down, folding him in her arms. "How was school?" she asks.

"Fine."

"Just fine? Anything happen?"

"No." Ben snuggles in.

"Nothing? All day?"

"Mama," he says. Ben very rarely calls her that anymore.

"Hmm?"

"I dreamed about Grammy B. last night."

Kate startles at the mention of her. "You did?"

"She said she didn't know where to go."

"What do you mean?"

"I don't know." Ben's eyes are big and bright, his face heart shaped.

"Then what?" she asks him.

"That's all. She was wearing her purple coat."

The purple coat. Her mother had worn that coat for as long as Kate could remember. Why had Ben dreamed about her?

"Hey, how about I order pizza?" she asks.

"Yeah!" Both boys shout simultaneously.

Kate gives Ben a squeeze and jumps up to find the phone. Extra pizza ordered. Might as well have leftovers for the weekend. David isn't due home until later tonight. Maybe a movie for Peter and Ben. Then she'll have some time to write. Or maybe take a long bath.

Kate can't help thinking about her childhood. Thank goodness Rachel had been born. She can't imagine not having that connection. They are true touchstones. Both had become estranged from their brother. How many times had friends not even known she had a brother? It was just too hard to explain. Maybe someday that would change.

"Should I put in a movie?" Kate calls to the boys.

"Yeah!" Ben's always up for a movie.

"Ah, maybe," says Peter. "When the pizza comes."

"No, now!"

"Fine," Peter relents. "I just finished my book."

"Good for you, Peter!" She can hardly get him to open a book. Then when he's into one, she can hardly get him to put it down. The doorbell rings.

"Pizza!" screams Ben.

That was fast. Probably not too many people order so early. She places slices onto plates and stirs chocolate milk. Perfect kid meal. Both boys are thrilled, and she pops in the movie. All Kate wants now is a bath. Alone time. When she was younger, especially during college, she couldn't stand being by herself. Always surrounded with friends, most of them with large personalities. Why?

Running the bath . . . taking off her clothes . . . an unexpected wave of sensuality runs through her. Kate slips into the water. Warmth envelops her. Things may really be changing . . .

A man's voice downstairs startles her. She listens carefully. David. Why is he home so soon? Maybe he'll spend some time with the boys.

• • •

With Ben finally asleep and Peter at least in his room for the night with his door closed, Kate looks for David.

"You here?" she asks the TV room. No answer. "David?"

"Down here." His voice is muffled. The basement. Kate walks downstairs. There he sits, at the computer, playing gin.

"You want to watch something?" she asks.

"Huh?"

Kate touches his shoulder, gently stroking his hair. "Want to do something?"

"I'm . . . no . . . I'm just . . . in the middle of a game." This David is all too familiar.

"Okay. I'll be upstairs. Come up soon?"

He doesn't answer. He probably didn't even hear her. She climbs back upstairs. Old feelings flood through her. Why had she thought he could change? Her thoughts slip easily into their well-worn grooves.

Kate waits up for hours. David never does come up. She cries herself to sleep.

Jennifer

Jennifer steps back, taking in the entire canvas. The form before her seems the shadow of a woman. Ghostly. Barely visible. Painted in midnight blue. Jennifer backs up even further. The woman is surrounded with increasingly lighter shades of blue. Is she falling? Emerging?

"Are you okay?" A woman stands, medium height, with dark curly hair, olive skin, and dancing almond eyes. "You looked a bit off there," she continues. Her voice is soothing, almost musical.

"Yeah." Jennifer realizes she's been staring. "Do I know you?"

The woman shakes her head. "Don't think so. But I'm here Fridays now. Have you been in before?"

"No. It's my first time." Jennifer looks around the room. Huge paintings cover the walls. It's a small, intimate gallery. "I love it."

"We're having a special showing next week. My work. You should come." The woman takes a postcard from a pile on the table nearby and hands it to Jennifer. "Think about it."

Jennifer looks down at a watercolor of a tree. It stands in the middle of what looks like an ocean of stars. The colors are deep blues. And an almost white yellow. It's stunning. Then she sees the woman's name.

"Anika Nappal?"

"Ana for short. Hope you can make it!" She turns and walks into the back room.

Jennifer leaves the gallery. It's dusk. She's hungry and doesn't feel like cooking. Chloe and Jimmy are with James for the night. Every Thursday and Friday night, and Tuesday afternoon. It works better than she'd feared. James agreed the children were better off with her most of the time. At least while they're so young. She would have been devastated if he'd fought her.

Maybe she should call Betty. She hasn't seen her in months. Jennifer feels a pang of guilt. She unzips the outer pocket of her purse and finds her cell phone. Thank God for that phone. It feels like a lifeline to her children when they're not with her.

"Hello?"

"Betty!"

"Oh! That you, Jen?"

"Yeah." Jennifer lets out an awkward laugh. "I know this is last minute, but you want to get some dinner?"

"I sure would, but I already ate. I'll come watch you stuff your face, though!"

"Sounds great."

"Where and when?"

Jennifer thinks. Mexican? Italian? "How about the Thai place?"

"I'll be there. What time?"

"I'll head over now. Just come when you're ready."

"Perfect," Betty responds. "I'll change, put on my face, and be right over."

"Okay. See you."

"Bye!"

Put on her face. As long as she's known Betty, she's used that phrase. And Jennifer had only seen her once without makeup, when she was really sick with the flu.

"Howdy, stranger!"

Jennifer looks up from her noodles. "Betty!" She scoots off her bench and gives Betty a hug.

"Long time no see!"

"I know," Jennifer says, embarrassed. "I'm so sorry. It's been crazy." It has been. She also hadn't felt like calling.

Betty slides into the seat across from her. "How's the pad thai?"

"Good. Want some?"

"No, no. I'm eating early and not that much lately." Betty pats her stomach. "Want to drop a few pounds before Florida."

"When is that?"

"Two weeks. And I've got seven to go."

"You look fabulous." Jennifer's glad she means it.

"I'm hoping to wear my bikini."

Jennifer smiles. "Drink?"

"That I can do." Betty points to Jennifer's water. "No wine?"

"I don't feel like it."

At that moment, the waitress comes over. "Anything for you?"

"I'll have a glass of white wine," Betty answers.

The waitress turns to Jennifer.

"No, thanks."

The waitress nods and leaves the table.

"So . . ." Betty places her hands on the table, palms down. "How are things?"

"Well," Jennifer begins, "in general, really good."

"The kids with James?"

"Yep. Two nights a week and one afternoon."

"Not bad! And they're all right?"

"They are," she says. "I mean, things come up. But things always come up with kids. I have to be careful not to think every little thing is about the divorce."

Betty's drink arrives, and she takes a sip. "And with James?"

Jennifer shrugs. "Not great, and not bad." She thinks of the drop-off the day before. "We're cordial. And kind. I think we both get that it's about the kids now. Chloe said something last week about a woman. I think he's seeing someone. Nothing serious, though."

"Not surprising. Men don't take long. They don't like to be alone." Betty sips her wine. "And you?"

Jennifer shakes her head.

"No one?"

"Nope."

"Not even so and so?"

"No." Definitely not him. "I've seen him around. He's with someone. Which is good. Our time has passed."

"It happens." Betty nods. "You seem . . . Actually, you seem better than I've ever seen you."

Jennifer's face feels hot. "Yeah. I guess I am. I mean, it's not easy. I've cried a ton—especially seeing Chloe's confusion. But you know what? I think you're right. And Chloe does better when I'm doing well. So, it's a huge incentive."

"Good job, Jen."

"Thanks. I know I've been out of touch. I've needed—I still need—a lot of space. Time to myself."

"Hey, you do what you need to do. Don't worry about me. Your kids come first. You come first. They're nothing without their mama." She drinks. "This wine isn't great."

Jennifer reaches for her water and has a sip. Her neck feels hot too.

"How's little Jimmy?"

"Oh, he's doing really well. Loves being at the big kids' school."

"I bet. Chloe keep an eye on him?"

Jennifer nods. "She's more protective of him now. It's sweet. And he loves it."

"What a good girl."

"Yeah. I'm so grateful. For a lot, actually. I mean, I still have tons of questions. But I don't feel like I'm fighting for my life. My sanity."

"You went through an awful lot." Betty nods.

"I did." Jennifer feels tired all of a sudden.

"You all right?"

"Yeah. I think . . . I'm so sorry, Betty. You just got here. I guess I've been a little off this afternoon. I thought I was fine, but I think I need to lie down."

They ask for the check, which Jennifer insists on paying. After hugging Betty good-bye outside the restaurant, Jennifer takes in the fresh night air. She looks up to see a perfect sky. All the stars sparkle.

● ● ●

Jennifer thinks about the dark tree in the painting on the postcard as she falls into a deep sleep. Trees and stars. Ana's dancing eyes.

Kate

Sessions with Marta have become something to look forward to. "I always thought I'd have a girl."

"Do you wish you had?"

"No," says Kate. "I used to. Not anymore, though. I think maybe I got off easy. No teenage daughter."

Marta laughs, then grows serious. "It's a very specific dynamic. Mother-daughter."

Kate doesn't want to go there. Not today. "I've been thinking about the bus."

"How so?"

"I *got on* that bus, Marta."

"Yes."

"That was four years ago, and I still feel like I'm processing it."

"That was when you started writing?" asks Marta.

"Yeah. *Because* of it. I didn't know what to do. How to integrate that experience with the me I was used to."

"Sometimes there are things in life that are so big, they can only be dealt with creatively," she offers. "It's as if we take them in slowly, and only over time do we grasp their meaning. How do you feel about it now?"

"Well, when it was happening, I was just in it. Then, later, I started to have questions. And now . . . I still think, *Who was that woman?*"

"Is it possible you glimpsed something in yourself . . . and are slowly moving toward that vision?"

"It is . . ." Kate nods. Maybe she's catching up to herself. "I feel like I still don't know."

"I would encourage you to keep trusting yourself and the process."

"I'm terrible with patience."

"I understand." Marta smiles compassionately. "It took me a long time to understand that impatience can equal a lack of trust."

"Wow. I never would've thought of that." Kate thinks about Peter and Ben. "I have a lot of patience with the boys. Not so much with myself. You know, the character I'm writing about has a daughter."

"Yes? And what else does she have?"

Kate has only recently begun to share a bit more about her writing with Marta, feeling herself increasingly immersed in the story. "She has a lot going on. Including a limited husband. Like David . . ."

"We all have limitations. There can be something profoundly absent, but that doesn't mean he's not trying."

"Doesn't feel like it."

"Did something happen, Kate?"

"Nothing new." She shrugs. "I thought things were changing."

Marta speaks softly. "David may be doing the best he can. No one will be present every moment. I think it's important you not give him so much power."

"What do you mean?"

"What if he's less relevant? Sometimes he'll meet you, other times he won't. You continue to do your thing. Your writing, your mothering . . ."

"Hmm," Kate takes it in. "But sometimes I feel so upset."

"I know, and I understand. Don't give him so much of your focus. You have your creative work."

"So, I let him off the hook?"

"No . . . just let him hang there."

Kate laughs.

"I say that for effect." Marta smiles. "Keep coming back to yourself."

"Okay." Kate stares at Marta's painting. This is about more than David . . . "I'm actually wondering something."

"About?"

"My upbringing. And what you said just now about how much focus I give David."

"Go on . . ."

"Well, my childhood, the community I grew up in, the fellowship . . . I think it had a huge impact on me, in a way I'm just now starting to see."

"How so?" Marta is curious.

"I've always been aware of so many good things about that experience. Especially in our household. The grown-ups really loved us kids, and we had a lot of fun. Not every household was like that, so we were lucky. But the leaders of the fellowship were all men. The elders. And I think there's something deep in me, in my unconscious even, where I give men a kind of authority."

"Can you say more?"

"I just recently started to see something in my writing. With my main female character and how caught up she is listening to the men in her life. To what they're saying. Wanting to please them. It's taken an incredible amount for her to even begin to hear herself."

"That is quite something."

"I'm starting to realize I'm like that. Like her. I think it has to do with the elders. And how I am, somehow, with David."

Marta nods slowly, pausing before she responds. "I believe you're getting to the heart of something important. You combine religion and patriarchy; you've got a loaded gun on your hands."

"Totally."

"And"—Marta thinks for a moment—"we may want to talk more about your relationship with your father at some point."

Kate shifts in her chair.

"I know you weren't close."

"No . . ."

"It doesn't need to be today," Marta continues. "I am curious, though, about the man who ran the workshop you went to recently. Since we're looking at the male voice. What of his?"

"Oh, you're wondering if he fits that pattern. If I give him authority over me."

"It's worth asking yourself."

"I'd say no. He has a softer way about him. And he actually gave a lot of space for the women in the group in terms of participation. I noticed that."

"Good," Marta states simply.

"Oh—I got a few more books he wrote. I'm reading one now about dreaming, and life after death."

"How is that?"

"He talks about how a lot of people start to pay more attention to dreams because of contact with a loved one who has died." Kate's eyes widen. "And there's even a way to work with and assist the spirit of someone who has passed. He calls it a 'facilitation to the other side.'"

"Very interesting."

Kate sighs. "Everything feels different for me now."

"How is that?"

"I don't know. I don't feel so worried about what other people think."

"Isn't that a great feeling?" Marta must have come to this place a long time ago.

"It is."

"Well, it may be that clarity of purpose will come with time."

Kate nods.

"And your writing?"

"I'm really into it. I think I'm three-fourths of the way."

"Wow. Good for you!"

"Will you read it when I'm done?" Kate says on impulse, surprising herself.

"I'd love to. You just let me know."

"Thank you. That means so much to me." Kate suddenly remembers something she wanted to bring up this session. "And, Marta?"

"Yes?"

"There's one more thing I want to quickly say, about my mother. I know we don't have time to get into it."

"Go on."

"My mother was in Ben's dream recently. And then in mine. It was so real."

"What happened?"

"She comes into my room and kneels by my bed. Creepy. Honestly, I could almost feel her breath on me." Kate notices the time. "Oh, sorry. I didn't mean to go over."

"No, this is good. See what comes up for you this week, particularly around 'mother.' In your writing too. It may be important to talk about further. Also, what you brought up about the elders."

Why had Kate talked about the very things she wanted to avoid?

● ● ●

KATE KNOCKS THREE TIMES AND CRACKS THE DOOR OPEN. "Hey! I'm here."

"Come on in!" Nia yells from the other room. "Do you want red or white?"

"White! Every time I come over, I fall more in love with your place." The vibrant reds and oranges are an exquisite contrast to the natural tones. Nia's luxury condo is spacious. Sophisticated. Kate regrets never having lived on her own. She had always had roommates. Then David.

Nia emerges from the kitchen with two glasses of white wine. She slowly and deliberately holds one out to Kate with her left hand . . .

Kate screams. "Oh my God!"

The ring is beautiful.

Nia grins ear to ear. "Joseph asked me to marry him!"

"It's absolutely gorgeous! Look at that diamond!"

"Joseph's grandmother's ring. It has been in the family for a long time."

"It's the most beautiful ring I've ever seen! Oh my God!" Kate screams again and throws her arms around Nia.

"I know!"

Kate squeezes her tight and then pulls back. "When did he propose?"

"Last night."

"Where?"

"We were at his place, and it was perfect. Joseph cooked a delicious dinner and had all these candles lit. And, Kate, when he started to get down on one knee . . . I honestly . . . I don't know how I didn't faint . . . I was so happy. And he was so sweet . . . just the way he asked me. I can hardly remember what he said in the beginning, and then he asked me, so formally, with those gorgeous big eyes, if I would marry him."

"You're getting married!"

"Yes!"

"To Joseph!"

"To the man of my dreams."

"How do you feel?"

"Tired . . . I hardly slept last night. I called my parents, Monique . . ."

Kate looks at the couch and moves a pillow to the side. "Sit."

They flop down together, setting down their glasses.

"And—" Nia's smile seems to illuminate her entire being. "I'm absolutely exhilarated."

"Oh, Nia!" Kate holds Nia's hand in hers.

"I'm about to get married to the most kind and thoughtful man."

"Your fiancé! Whoa—when is the wedding?"

"Three months."

"Three months?" Kate asks.

"Joseph and I don't want to wait to start our lives together. We want to be together and build a family." The way she says Joseph's name . . . So fondly.

"A family!"

"Can you believe it?" Nia's joy is contagious.

"Yes. It's phenomenal!"

"I was up half the night talking to Monique. I told her, and she's my maid of honor. She was screaming through the phone and was so excited. And then we started crying together because she's halfway across the world and just got this massive promotion. There's no way she can get away from her project." Nia lays her other hand on Kate's. "Will you stand in as my maid of honor?"

Kate and Nia both begin to cry.

"I would be deeply honored."

"We really want it to be an intimate wedding and reception with the closest of the close family and friends we have."

"It sounds so lovely."

Kate's eye catches the ornate print on Nia's wall. A watercolor of two women dancing, each in a different stage of the dance. One woman with her arms stretched upward, opening. The other lowering her arms, cradling what is to come.

"Nia, I am so happy for you."

"I am the happiest I have ever been."

● ● ●

Kate looks up to see David standing in the doorway.

"Doing some writing?" he asks, then notices. "On the computer!"

"Yeah."

"Don't you miss your notebook?" he teases.

"Ha! No." Kate turns her attention back to the keyboard. In these creative bursts, her writing feels more real than her own life.

"Want to watch a movie?"

"I don't know," she answers. "I'm right in the middle . . ."

"Okay." David starts to leave.

"I'm . . . constantly surprised by these characters. I never know what's about to happen . . . then the words come through. Like it's writing itself."

David leans against the wall. "That's the best way to write. Keep going. You're on a roll."

"Yeah." The story has taken over lately. The end may be nearing.

SPLIT OPEN

Kate doesn't realize until she tiptoes upstairs late, quietly undresses, and slips under the covers, that earlier that evening, David had come to her. Wanting to be with her. And it was she who was busy. Unavailable.

Kate curls into him. Smiling.

Jennifer

There's magic in the air. She can feel it. All week, Jennifer has looked forward to tonight.

"Jimmy! Chloe! Come have some pizza!" She ordered their favorite, half pepperoni with double cheese.

"Coming!" Chloe yells from her room.

"Pizza, pizza, pizza!" Jimmy races into the kitchen. "Gimme two pieces!"

Jennifer laughs and lays two plain cheese slices on his plate. "How was your day, sweetie?"

"Can I have chocolate milk?"

"I don't know." Jennifer considers. "You're going to Daddy's, remember? In an hour. You usually have ice cream over there, right?"

"And a movie."

"So how about plain milk?"

Jimmy sighs. "Okay."

"You know, you're looking taller these days."

"Daddy has a measuring stick."

"Really?"

"Yep." Jimmy lights up. "And I grew an inch."

"Wow! That's crazy!" Jennifer opens the refrigerator and finds the milk. She takes a glass from the dish drainer and fills it halfway.

"Chloe?" she calls. "Come on! You want milk?"

"Water." Chloe walks into the kitchen. "I'm starved."

"Have as much as you want."

"We go to Dad's tonight, right?" Chloe sounds surprisingly grown-up. She takes three pieces of pepperoni.

"That's right. Pretty soon."

"Where'd he go, anyway?"

"Yeah," Jimmy echoes.

"New York."

"For work?" Chloe's mouth is so full, she barely gets the words out.

Jennifer gives her a look. "Yes. Chloe . . ."

"Sorry. I couldn't help it." Still chewing. "By the way, I love my desk. It's perfect."

Jennifer beams. "Good!" Along with seeming more grown-up, Chloe is back to her old eating habits.

"You look nice." Chloe looks at her mother.

"Pretty," Jimmy agrees.

Jennifer blushes.

Chloe gasps, a look of horror on her face. "Do you have a date?"

"No, sweetness. I don't. I'm going to an art opening after I take you and Jimmy to your dad's."

"What's that?" asks Jimmy.

"It's a place to see artwork," Chloe responds in her matter-of-fact way. "I know from school. We've been studying different artists. We're having our own exhibit in two weeks. You can come. Dad too."

"Really?" asks Jennifer. It's the first she's heard of it. "When?"

"We're making invitations. I'll bring it next week."

"Oh, sweetie, I can't wait to see your work."

"Thanks." Chloe smiles.

"I draw too!" Jimmy boasts.

"This is painting, Jimmy." Chloe's tone verges on snooty. "There's a difference."

"I know!" Jimmy shouts at his sister. "I've been painting ever since preschool!"

"Okay, guys, that's enough. And yes, you have, Jimmy. Quite well, I might add."

He sticks his tongue out at Chloe. She one-ups him by opening her mouth full of pizza. Jennifer is suddenly more than ready for a night off. An evening of adults and art.

"More milk."

Jennifer pours him a bit more. "Chloe? More water?"

"No. I'm done." She stands. "Can I go?"

"Yes. You ate that fast enough."

"I have to do something. When do we leave?"

Jennifer checks the clock. "We should get ready. Twenty minutes." She needs to see how her hair dried. Maybe put on some lipstick.

"Okay. Get me when it's time." Chloe walks to her room, closing the door.

"All right." *So independent. It's good, Chloe doing her own thing.*

"Mommy?" *No more Mama?*

"Yeah?"

"I dreamed last night that Daddy went away—and never came back."

"Oh, Jimmy." Jennifer lays her hand on his back. "How'd that make you feel?"

"Sad." He shrugs.

"Come here." She folds her arms around him. "That sounds so sad. Are you worried?"

"I don't know." He looks down.

"Well, you don't need to be. Daddy loves you and Chloe so much. And he and I talked about how important it is that we stay in the same place."

"Okay." Jimmy doesn't seem upset.

"You really okay?"

"Yep. Just want to get my red baseball hat. Daddy said we could play catch."

Jennifer releases her hug. "All right. Go get it."

What a sweet boy. It's something how he moves with ease from one moment to the next. Jennifer closes the pizza box and puts it in the refrigerator, along with the milk. *Time to switch gears.*

She walks to her bedroom and stands in front of the full-length mirror. Her black skirt and sleeveless top look nice. Simple. Jennifer runs her hands through her hair. She used to spend so much time blow-drying it. That was long ago. She carefully applies lipstick. That act can feel so sensual. She blots her mouth with a tissue, looking closely at her face. The wrinkles around her eyes have deepened.

● ● ●

THERE'S A PARKING SPOT RIGHT IN FRONT OF THE GALLERY where someone has just pulled out. James was in a good mood when she dropped off Chloe and Jimmy. That relaxed her. Jennifer checks herself quickly in the rearview mirror. She grabs her small black purse from the passenger seat with her wallet, cell phone, and breath mints in it. Her regular purse is so clunky and full. Tonight, she feels light.

The room feels calm when she walks in.

"Welcome." A tall woman kindly greets Jennifer. "Care for a glass of wine?"

"I'd love one."

"White or red?"

"White, please."

The woman hands her one from a tray. "Enjoy."

"Thank you."

Jennifer takes a sip. Cold. Refreshing. She looks to her right. There hangs the six-foot painting from the postcard. Jennifer catches her breath. The tree, as black as night, stands boldly in the midst of bright stars. A swirling sea of every blue shade.

"Wow," she says under her breath.

"You like?"

She hadn't realized she'd spoken out loud.

"Ana, hi! I *love*."

"Thank you. I'm glad you came. Not still woozy, are you?"

"No." Jennifer laughs, embarrassed. "And thanks. Me too. Glad I came. Your painting is stunning. I hardly know what to say."

"Say you'll see the others. It's a series of four." She laughs. "I'll let you look at them in peace. I'll be over by the wine."

"I'll find you."

Jennifer takes in the paintings. Each one increases in lightness, to the point where the last is a dancing array of brilliant swirling reds and oranges. The stars replaced by a shining sun. Breathtaking. Only the tree remains the same—midnight black. As Jennifer glances back through the series, she sees that tiny buds emerge little by little in each. The final tree is in full bloom, with glorious white flowers.

Jennifer looks around. Ana stands talking to the woman with the tray. She looks up. Jennifer smiles. Ana comes toward her.

"These are the most strikingly beautiful paintings I've ever seen."

"Thank you. So much!"

"I mean it. Not that I'm a connoisseur or anything. But, Ana, they're very . . . special."

"Do you have a favorite?"

"I don't know." Jennifer considers. "They each capture a certain mood."

"I do." This woman seems so different.

"Which one?" Jennifer asks.

"You tell me first. Which brings you the deepest response?"

Jennifer looks at each painting. In order. Her eyes come back to the beginning, resting on the blue. "The first."

"And mine's the last. I think mainly because I could only get to it by going through all the others. I worked hard for it."

"I bet." Jennifer looks at Ana. "How long did these all take?"

"Four years. On and off."

"Wow. One painting per year?" Fascinating.

"Yes, that's it."

"How did you work on the same piece, the same image, for so long?"

"It called to me. And I had a lot to work through." Ana looks into Jennifer's eyes. "Someone I loved very much once told me that when one is 'in it,' creativity is the way through."

"That's so brave."

"Or completely mad." Ana laughs. "I am brave now. From this." What would it be like to be her? "I don't even know your name."

"Jennifer."

"That's my sister's name!" Ana grins. "My absolute favorite name."

Jennifer's cheeks flush as she brings her glass to her lips.

"I really am glad you came, Jennifer. I plan to show in New York. I'm in negotiations with a gallery in the Village. Tonight's my tiny premiere." Ana reaches into her pocket. "My personal card."

She places the card in Jennifer's hand. It has the image of the dark tree on the side, next to her name and number.

"Thank you."

Ana suddenly looks up. "Oh, I see my roommate and her fiancée."

"Go. Talk with them."

"Okay. I should. You can come. I'll introduce you."

"No, no. I should go. This is your night." Jennifer suddenly needs fresh air. "Thank you so much," she says in parting. "You are unbelievably talented."

"My pleasure. Hope you have a wonderful night."

"You too, Ana." Jennifer turns to go.

"Jennifer?"

"Yeah?"

"Call me. Even for a cup of coffee."

"I will." She smiles big as she exits the gallery. Jennifer slides Ana's card into her wallet. What was it about her? A fluidity. A strength. It's thrilling.

Kate

Ben stands in Kate's room. It's the middle of the night. She thinks it is David, then remembers he is still in New York.

"You have another bad dream?" Kate pulls Ben under the covers.

He snuggles close. "Grammy died."

Again. Why is he dreaming this? Kate is surprised Ben remembers her so vividly. It's been years since they saw her. So much hurt. Kate pushes her feelings away. She feels sorry for her mom, for her wounds. Yet could no longer accept the pain her mom inflicted on her. Her overwhelming emotional needs. Lack of boundaries. Kate finally felt she needed to set the ultimate boundary. No contact.

Marta said to open more to her feelings. To the hurt. But regarding her mother, Kate feels so much internal resistance. And confusion.

SPLIT OPEN

Why her fascination with life after death? Kate remembers her first research paper as a freshman in high school. She chose the topic of life after death. What an unusual choice for a fourteen-year-old. She also shared with Rachel, years ago, how she wondered why there are midwives for birth and not death.

This came up at the workshop. From the dream perspective, it is the shaman who acts as a bridge between worlds—journeying to acquire information or healing for the benefit of oneself or another. This can also happen while dreaming, a realm the shaman lives in and knows is real.

Ben. Wrapped in her embrace. His body jerks in his sleep a number of times. Kate hardly sleeps the rest of the night.

Kate jolts awake, out of breath. She must have been dreaming. Ben is still cradled in her arms. What a relief. Kate tries to steady herself. She dozes a little before light begins to creep in through the corners of the windows.

● ● ●

BEN FINALLY COMES DOWNSTAIRS.

"Mommy?"

Kate looks up from her book. Ben looks drained.

"Hey . . . come here. How are you?"

He sits heavily in her lap. "Tired."

She holds him.

Ben looks up. "Where's Peter?"

"School."

"I'm staying home?" He lays his head on her shoulder. "My tummy hurts."

Kate picks him up. "You want to watch TV?"

"Can I?"

"Yeah." She wants to distract him. He doesn't look good. "Want some 7UP?"

"In the morning?"

"How about just this once? For your tum."

Ben nods. After settling him onto the couch, Kate walks over to the coffeepot. She made more than usual this morning, knowing she would need it. She pours another cup. Ben is so open. Very much like her, especially when she was little. Kate's heart leaps. Was it her fault he's dreaming like this?

She sips her coffee. Maybe some cinnamon. She shakes some into her mug. She'll miss the walk she won't have today. And she planned to write until the boys came home from school. It will have to wait.

Wind gusts outside. A large oak tree sways back and forth. It reminds her of the print on Nia's wall. This is how the women seemed to move in their dance. The phone rings. Kate jumps.

"Hello?"

"Hey!"

"Hey! Wow, I was just thinking about you."

"I found my dress!" Nia sounds thrilled.

"You did?"

"I'm telling you, Kate, I walked past this window, and there it was. I wasn't looking or anything. I can't wait for you to see it. And here's the really unbelievable part: it fits me like it was made for me."

"What does it look like?"

"I'm not going to spoil the surprise. What is your afternoon like?"

"Oh, Nia, I'm so sorry, Ben is home sick today. And David's gone till tomorrow. I want to see it so bad!"

"Aww, I'm sorry Ben is sick."

"What about tomorrow?"

"That should work. I need to check on something, but let's call each other tonight or first thing in the morning, and we'll figure out a time."

"I can't wait to see it!"

"I seriously can't wait to show you. Okay, I need to go tackle about ten more things on my list."

"Perfect. I love you!"

"I love you, Kate. I'm getting married!"

"Aah!" Nia's dress! Nia's wedding!

Kate carries her empty mug to the sink. Might as well get some dishes done. She doesn't want the house to be a complete mess when David returns. It happens easily. Plus, she can watch the trees from the kitchen window.

The dishwater is warm and feels good. Kate's mind takes her to the huge tree at the workshop. She could have sat under it all day. And the black jaguar. She has felt the animal's presence increasingly since her dismemberment journey. What a powerful protector.

After doing the dishes, in spite of the coffee, Kate feels deeply tired. She needs to check on Ben. She fills two glasses with water.

Ben is sound asleep on the couch. Good. He needs it. Kate turns off the television and squeezes herself onto the other end of the couch, pulling the blanket carefully over Ben. Drifting . . .

• • •

"Ben's better?" David asks the following morning.

"Yes, thank goodness. That was a rough one." It feels good to have David back. "I took him to school today."

"Good. Come here." David holds her.

Kate relaxes in his arms. "Hey," she pulls back. "You call a therapist?"

"Oh yeah. I forgot. I will."

"Promise?"

"Yeah." David walks over to the wall calendar. "Is there anything going on tonight?"

"Can we watch a movie—as a family? Something funny. I need to laugh."

"Sounds good to me."

"And if I go to the store, will you make steak tonight?"

David raises an eyebrow. "Hungry jaguar?"

"Absolutely!"

"You got it. If you get the movie and steak, I'll cook it. I'm beat and need to get some work done."

Kate yawns. "I'm tired too."

"You'd better get your butt to the store," he teases.

"Okay, okay." She grabs her purse. "David?"

"Huh?"

"Am I the right wife for you?"

"What? Why are you asking that?"

Kate looks at the floor. She meant to sweep it. "I'm too weird."

"You," responds David, "are the perfect wife for me."

They share a smile.

"Hey," he adds, "I'm never bored!"

● ● ●

The moon is breathtaking. Completely full. Movie night is over, the boys are asleep, and David works in his office. Kate drinks her chamomile tea. What if Marta were her mother? She sets her tea down. What a thought.

Her mom had not been there. Not like she'd needed. Maybe the most painful part was how hidden it was, the emotional trespass. Kate had tried everything. At least she no longer has to manage her. It was emotionally exhausting. For so long.

And what about David's mother? Another woman who was unable to maintain healthy boundaries. Why couldn't she have ended up with a loving mother-in-law?

At least she hadn't been alone growing up. Maybe she would call Rachel. It's two hours earlier in Seattle. Yes, Rachel is exactly who she wants to talk to. Kate finishes the last sips of her lukewarm tea. Please be there . . .

"Hello?"

"Hi—" Kate immediately chokes up.

"Kate. You okay?" Rachel asks.

"I'm . . . Yeah. Sorry."

"No, it's fine. What's wrong?"

"Can you talk?"

"Yeah." She sounds concerned. "The boys okay?"

"Yes. Everything's fine. It's just . . . my own thinking. About Mom."

"Oh." There's a moment of silence.

"Why is she so hard?" Kate asks.

"She . . . You know, we were raised by a traumatized mother."

"I never thought about it like that. Those exact words. *Traumatized mother.*"

"It's intense." Rachel pauses. "I need a beer."

"Me too."

"Well, go get one," suggests Rachel. "I am, if we're really going there."

"Okay. Actually, I have wine open."

"Well, uncork that shit."

There's the sound of a bottle opening over the phone and Rachel drinking. Kate uncorks the red wine and pours some into her empty teacup.

"Okay." Rachel is all business. "Why're you thinking about Mom?"

"It's been a long week." Should she tell Rachel about Ben's dream? No. Not now. "I just all of a sudden wished Marta was my mother."

"I get that."

They sip their drinks.

"Know why you were smart?" Kate asks.

"Why?"

"You never let her in." Rachel had held their mother at arm's length.

"Yes." Rachel sighs. "I did."

"When?"

"When I had asthma."

"Oh."

"Mom would take care of me. It was complicated," Rachel continues. "I used to love the way she felt. Loved it! Big and comforting. Then that same bigness started to seep out, like a spill. Till I couldn't breathe."

"Yeah." Kate knows exactly.

"But I got smart."

"Yes, you did." Kate takes another sip. "Took me a lot longer."

"It was different for you. You had her grandchildren."

"I thought I was obligated."

"And you're the oldest."

"Like she is." Kate thinks a moment. "And then when Dad died, I feel like that's when she became really difficult. For me. Like he was her target, and when he wasn't there anymore, she turned to me."

There's a clinking sound.

"You opening another beer already?"

"Oh yeah. I don't mess."

"You know what was hardest?" Kate asks.

"What?"

"How invisible it was."

"True," Rachel agrees.

"Almost . . . insidious," Kate dares.

"That word isn't wrong." Rachel begins to laugh.

"What?"

"Remember—that time—with the piano?"

"Oh my God." Kate's stomach turns.

"How she was sucking us into her bizarre reality—"

"We were trapped!"

"Practically at gunpoint!" adds Rachel.

"Totally!" Kate's laughing hard.

"You were hiding in the kitchen!"

"Yeah—looking for anything alcoholic!"

"She was torturing us, Peter and Ben too, with her deranged singalong!" Rachel loses it. "Some old church song."

"I thought it"—Kate gasps for air—"was a nursery rhyme!"

"I don't remember!" Rachel shrieks. "It traumatized me! Oh, shit. And speaking of deranged. How about that guinea pig?"

"What guinea pig?"

There's a pause.

"What?" asks Rachel. "What do you mean?"

"I don't know. What do *you* mean?"

"That crazy-ass thing she killed."

"What?"

"You don't know this?" Rachel sounds stunned.

"No! What?"

"She took a psycho guinea pig from someone. A neighbor was getting rid of it or something. It bit people. And one day," Rachel continues, "it just disappeared."

"Where?"

"I asked Mom, and she acted really weird and wouldn't talk about it."

"Why?"

"I made it my mission to find out. I became obsessed with it." Rachel drinks. "Then, when she couldn't deal with my questions anymore, Mom said really calmly, you know how she would, 'Well, one day . . . I took the guinea pig and put it in a plastic bag . . . and closed it . . . and walked around for a while . . . and it very gently . . . just . . . went . . . to sleep.'"

Kate can't believe her ears. "No."

"Yes."

"No! Rachel! I don't even know what to say. That's so creepy!"

"It was," Rachel says, sounding matter-of-fact.

"I never saw her do anything like that."

"I think you were at college."

Kate shakes her head. "That's horrifying."

"It still freaks me out," says Rachel. "And she acted like I would lose interest about why the thing just disappeared. Like I was two or something. I was fourteen!"

A pause. "Can you imagine? A plastic bag?" Rachel starts laughing again.

"That's not funny!"

"I know!" Rachel grows quiet for a moment. "I will say one thing, though. In her defense."

"What?"

"That guinea pig was not right."

They burst into laughter.

"Had red eyes! And it wasn't albino."

"Thanks for making me laugh. I don't know what I'd do without you."

"You'd be not right too!" Rachel cracks up again. It takes a long time for the laughter to die down, then Rachel lets out a big sigh. "But really, it's hard for people to stay in a relationship with her for very long."

"Yeah. And it's especially devastating to cut off your own mother."

"I know. I can handle once in a while, but with Mom, you never quite know who you're dealing with."

"I know."

"Yeah. I used to wonder which Mom would show up," Rachel continues. "But the thing is, and what we had no way of understanding, is that her trauma made her act that way."

"The constant victim."

"Yep. With this continual feeling that someone's out to get her. But she actually had that experience when she was little. And then again to some extent in the fellowship."

"Exactly," Kate agrees.

Rachel lets out a breath. "It's complex."

"You know"—Kate runs her fingers through her hair—"no one would understand what we're talking about."

"I know. That's why I don't talk about her. Or Phillip."

"Me neither. Friends I've had for years don't know I have a brother. And with Mom, it's taken so long to get to where I could even begin to see her clearly."

"She isn't just one thing," Rachel says directly. "And . . . there were some really good things about her when we were little."

"True. I think I need to talk about her more in therapy. I've been putting her out of my mind."

"It might help. You should if you want. I also wonder . . ."

"What?" Kate asks.

"Well . . ." Rachel sounds hesitant. "I wonder if there might be a way you could have some sort of relationship with Mom. You know? Some sort of connection, but where you don't feel overwhelmed by her."

"I've tried." Over and over. "She's different with me than you. I don't know why. She just won't honor any kind of boundary with me."

"I know," says Rachel softly. "I just wonder about . . . how you'll feel . . . when one day she's gone. I don't want you to have regrets."

Ben's dreams. And her own recently.

"Yeah."

"Just think about it," she offers. "No pressure. Just see . . ."

"Okay. I'll at least bring it up to Marta."

"Sounds good."

"I love you."

"I love you too, Kate."

Kate drags herself upstairs and flops into bed.

Jennifer

FULL-MOON MISCHIEF. MEMORIES OF WILD NIGHTS LONG AGO. Jennifer refills her vase, thinking of Ana. She had been nervous to call her. But their coffee went great. Being around Ana makes her feel like she can do anything. Jennifer sets fresh flowers in the middle of her little rustic table. She had gotten it for next to nothing at a yard sale. She had bargained for, or found on sale, almost every piece in her apartment.

Jennifer takes in the whole room. Transformed from functional to chic. It had been a joy bringing it all together. Sparked a creativity she hasn't felt since childhood.

At coffee, Ana had invited her to a party the following Friday. Jennifer was thrilled it fell on her free weekend night. She's getting to know Ana. She knows Ana went to art school, then dropped out to join a band. She studies Buddhism and meditates as regularly as she can. She is younger than Jennifer.

Single. No kids. And wants to go to New York. Make a living as a painter. She also loves to dance. Jennifer promised they would go dancing sometime soon.

• • •

"That's mine." Chloe points proudly to her painting, hanging on her classroom wall. "It's a self-portrait." She looks at Jimmy. "That means it's me."

"I know," he responds.

"Oh, sweetie." Jennifer loves it. "It's incredible!"

The face in the painting looks happy.

"And that too." Chloe points. "And those."

Jennifer and Jimmy take their time, looking over all the artwork.

"These are really spectacular, Chloe. When did you do them?"

"The whole year. We've been saving them, for our exhibition." She looks toward the door. "When's Dad coming?"

"I don't know. He said he'd be here. Oh, sweetheart, this one's stunning." Jennifer stares at a watercolor of a butterfly. Full of bright color and life.

"Daddy!" Jimmy yells.

The whole room looks. Jennifer smiles, a bit embarrassed. Everyone knows they are divorced by now. Still, these school functions make her feel self-conscious.

"My boy!" James hugs Jimmy with one arm and holds out the other to Chloe. "How's my artist?"

"Good." She beams. "Come see!" Chloe pulls him over to her area. Each child has a part of the room set up with their own work. As James passes Jennifer, he nods to her. He looks tired, but his smile is genuine. His eyes soft. What a contrast to a year ago.

"I need to go to the bathroom." Jimmy grabs Jennifer's hand.

"Okay, go on."

"Come with."

"You go at school every day. I'll be right here."

"No, come," he begs.

"All right."

Jennifer holds his hand. Her little big-boy. It might be good to give Chloe a few minutes alone with James. Turning, she almost runs right into Lily's mother.

"Oh, hi!"

"I'm so sorry," Jennifer responds automatically. "How are you?"

"Good, good. And you?"

"Good!" It feels nice it feels true.

"Is Chloe in there?"

"Yeah."

"Lily was looking for her. We'll see you later." Plastic smile.

Jimmy comes out of the bathroom and takes Jennifer's hand, pulling her toward the playground.

"I want to swing! Just for a minute! Please? Pretty please?"

"Oh, all right." Jennifer laughs. "Just till Chloe comes."

Jimmy squeals with delight. He loves swinging. Jennifer gives him a high underdog. He could swing for hours. She looks to see Chloe and James walking toward them.

"You want me to come back in with you?" Jennifer asks.

"No, you saw everything." Chloe is glowing from the attention. "Can we get ice cream? Dad said . . ."

James looks sheepish. "I said it's okay if your mom says it is."

Jimmy screams, "Ice cream!"

"Well, I guess we'd better," Jennifer says as she laughs. "You both coming in my car?"

"No, I'm going with Daddy!" Jimmy, so excited.

"I'll go with you, Mom." Chloe shrugs.

"Okay," says Jennifer, "but not too long. It's late."

● ● ●

"Strawberry, please." Chloe eyes the pink container. "In a sugar cone."

Jennifer nudges Jimmy. "Umm . . ." His eyes are wide. Searching. "Umm . . ."

The woman behind the counter hands Chloe her cone.

"How about mint chip?" Jennifer suggests.

"Yeah! Mint chip," Jimmy echoes. That's what he usually wants, even if he chooses something else.

"Cup or cone?" the woman asks.

"Cup."

She scoops the ice cream and hands the cup to Jimmy.

"I'll have a scoop of double fudge chocolate. In a plain cone." Jennifer turns to James. "You having some?"

He shakes his head. "My stomach."

"Oh. Sorry."

"Ever since New York. Too much spicy food. And yeast. I'm cutting out wheat and dairy."

"How long?"

"Ma'am?" The woman hands Jennifer her cone.

"I got it." James has his wallet out and pays for the ice cream.

"Thanks."

Chloe looks so happy. "Come sit with us."

It will be the first time they've sat together as a family. Since the divorce. Jennifer slides in next to Jimmy. James sits by Chloe.

"So?" Jennifer looks at James.

"What?"

"How long with no dairy? And no wheat. That's hard."

"Yeah. I'm trying to do all month." He turns to Chloe. "But you're not making it easy for me to resist!" He lunges toward her ice cream.

"Daddy!" She pulls her cone away, giggling. He smiles triumphantly. He got a *Daddy* out of her.

"Your art exhibit was very impressive." Jennifer leans in. "I can tell you worked hard on those paintings."

"I like the butterfly," Jimmy pipes up.

Jennifer puts her arm around him. "Me too," she says.

"Dad?" Chloe looks to her father expectantly.

"Well," he thinks a moment, "I like the one of the big house and the flowers. But my very favorite . . ."

"Was of me and you!" Chloe completes his sentence.

Jennifer feels a slight pang. "I didn't see that."

"I showed him just for special. It's in my desk."

"And," adds James, "I get to have it at the end of the year."

"For his office!" she exclaims.

"Maybe I'll frame it."

Chloe lights up. "Yeah!"

Their family is slowly finding a new way to come together. Jennifer looks at James. He is a good father. His devotion to

Chloe and Jimmy has increased over their months apart. How fortunate to know they're well cared for when they are with him.

"Thank you," she says.

"What?" He gives her a quizzical look.

"The ice cream." Jennifer smiles. "And a good night."

"A great night!" Chloe declares.

Suddenly, Jennifer has to stop herself from bursting into tears. It catches her off guard. Chloe's special night was a success. Chloe will have many questions about relationships as she grows older. Such a vulnerable thing to become a young woman. And, really, the vulnerability never ends. Yet there is strength too.

"Hey, guys." Jennifer looks at her watch. "We should get going."

Time to go home.

Kate

KATE GLANCES ONCE MORE AT THE CROWD BEFORE FINALLY standing up. She holds her champagne glass in one hand, holds the other over her heart, and turns to her best friend.

"Nia, it has been my genuine privilege to know you ever since third grade." Kate glances again at the crowd, then says to Nia, "I used to love jumping rope like everyone else, but then . . . I'll never forget walking outside at recess and seeing you Double Dutch! You absolutely blew my mind! I watched from the sidelines—and one day you invited me in. And that's when our friendship started. Until this very day, I will never forget that you're the one who taught me"—Kate chants rhythmically—"'Teddy bear, teddy bear, turn all around. Teddy bear, teddy bear, *touch* the ground!' I didn't think I could do it, but you told me I could. And I did. You taught me how to touch the ground—and you still do."

Kate tilts her head slightly and looks at the crowd. "You may not all know this, but Nia was the 'Double Dutch Recess Queen'! And every Friday, I got to be the 'Double Dutch Queen's Assistant'!"

Everyone laughs, and a few people even clap. Kate feels the knot in her stomach begin to loosen. She leans back toward her friend.

"Nia, I thought you were the most beautiful girl in the whole world, and it still holds true. This day proves me right."

Nia beams. Kate looks back at the crowd. "Now, me and everyone else here knows how close Nia and Monique are and always will be. She would have flown in from her huge work project in South Korea, but just couldn't make it. As sad as we are not to have Monique here to make this toast, I am absolutely honored to be standing in for her right now. I've known many of you for years, and you've made me feel like part of your family. And here stand Joseph and Nia, in front of their closest family and friends, as husband and wife."

Kate unexpectedly chokes up. She takes a deep breath. "Joseph and Nia, you have come together in the most genuine, adoring, and devoted way—by seeing and embracing the light and love in one another. It is my true honor to toast you on this glorious day—the most elegant wedding I have ever witnessed. I admire the strength and beauty of your love and celebrate your divine union. I love you." Kate holds her glass high. "May your blessings continue to unfold!"

Everyone toasts.

Nia mouths, *I love you too.*

Kate sits and takes a huge swig of champagne. There's clapping and whistles from the crowd. Dizzying. She did it. What a relief. Another sip. Kate feels someone touch her back, then her waist. David.

"You were superb! Sounded great."

"Thanks! I was so nervous."

"I couldn't tell." He looks down. "Except you just drank all your champagne in one gulp."

"Oh my. I did!"

"More?"

"Definitely."

He pours her another glass and refreshes his own.

Kate feels palpably aware of both their joy and sorrow. How complex a marriage is. Only by holding through it is it possible for those dimensions to find their way, sometimes through great struggle, to something new. She had no idea what lay ahead the day she married David.

"Your speech was very moving."

"Really?" Kate touches his cheek. "You are more handsome than the day we married."

"With that haircut? I hope so!"

"Really. You are."

"And you," David takes her hand in his, "are radiant."

Nia and Joseph head for the dance floor. Their first dance.

"Remember ours?" asks David.

"I sure do." So many dances within a marriage . . .

• • •

KATE SMILES AT MARTA.

"I think I want to do more training. You know how people say things like, 'I haven't been the same since,' or 'I lost a part of myself,' when they've gone through something? A trauma? Or what feels traumatic?"

Marta nods.

"From the dreaming and shamanic perspective," Kate continues, "that's literal. Part of a person's essence, or soul, can break off and leave. For different reasons. And it's possible to call that part back. Through soul retrieval."

"Hmmm." Marta thinks a moment. "I feel I have seen this also in my work."

"I'm sure you have." Kate takes in Marta's presence. "Sometimes I think of you because it seems like you work in these realms. You just do it differently."

"Could be. I find this soul retrieval concept"—she pauses—"interesting. There does seem to be something in there for you. As long as you know *you* are in charge of your life."

Kate nods. "I'm really working on it. More than ever. And that's a huge part of it—that you are your own best teacher."

"Yes. There are a lot of people out there on ego trips, claiming to be this or that. It's important to be discerning."

"Absolutely."

"And David? Where is he with all of this?"

"Well . . ." Kate thinks about their most recent conversation. "He doesn't pretend to get it. It's not his thing. But what's interesting is there are ways this invisible work is being made visible to him."

"That must be quite an experience for him." Marta squints.

"Yeah, well, it's not easy. For either of us."

"So, he's supportive?"

"He is."

Marta smiles. "I'm glad."

"But," says Kate, "I'm also seeing something. About David."

"Yes?"

"He's not going to make that call. To a therapist."

"Well, that is his choice." Marta's response is surprising.

"But he promised."

"Yes. I know. And maybe he will in time. And maybe not."

Kate gives Marta a look.

"You may simply need to accept David for who he is."

Kate sits back, folding her arms across her stomach.

"And his support," Marta continues. "What if both are true? He supports you in your growth. And doesn't choose to go there himself. That is his right."

Something begins to shift with this thought. "I'm starting to get it."

"You sound surprised."

"I am. I'm so used to feeling hurt by him. Wanting him to do more."

"And by accepting who he is, you can get on with your life. Go to your training. Do your writing. Be you."

Kate nods enthusiastically.

"How's that going?"

"My writing?"

"Mm-hmm."

Her heart speeds up. "I'm almost done."

"How exciting!"

"Yeah. I can't believe it."

"Good for you!"

"Thanks!" Kate relishes Marta's support. "I love it. I never would've guessed how much joy I'd find in it." Kate thinks about her writing. How far she has come.

"That is the value of creative work," says Marta.

"Yeah."

"It's not about the product. Simply the love of the process itself."

"That's it. And," Kate says, "I feel like I've found something in myself somehow through this story."

"That is really wonderful. Quite a change from when I first met you."

Kate thinks back to her first session with Marta. "So true."

"You're coming into your own."

"Thank you, Marta."

"You should feel proud of yourself."

"I'm glad I had no idea where it was going when I began. How hard it would be."

"Sometimes it's best not to know where we're headed."

"If I'd known . . . so many things . . ."

"Yes." Then Marta unexpectedly asks, "How are you feeling about your mother now?"

"Well, I . . . actually, I had a good conversation with my sister about her."

"Yes?"

"I've been crying. A lot. Mourning her, in a way. How she isn't who I want my mom to be."

"Oh . . . yes. It may take time. There is much grieving before one is able to accept deep disappointment." They are silent for a bit.

"She was really hurt when she was little. Sexually abused by her grandfather. She told me when I was sixteen. And . . ."

Marta is patient.

"And," Kate continues, "the first words out of my mouth were, 'I knew it.' Which wasn't really true. I didn't know. But it somehow explained this thing I felt in my bones about her. Something that didn't feel right, and I could never quite put my finger on."

"Yes . . ."

"And I found out much later that when I was around six, right around when I started wetting my bed, she had shared the abuse with my dad and the elders in the fellowship. And then she was looked at differently. As being bad or damaged."

"Hurt again . . . by the elders? And possibly even her own husband?"

Kate nods. Such deep trauma. "I just want her to be okay. Not a victim. Not someone who has always wanted to somehow—devour me."

"Oh," Marta says so gently.

"Why wouldn't she just do her work and get better?"

Marta lets Kate's words hang in the air. "It's possible," she slowly offers. "It's not that she wouldn't. It could very well be that she *couldn't*."

Kate stares at her.

"And that can be incredibly painful to accept."

Kate is dumbfounded. "I never thought of that."

"And it could be also that David did not choose the way he is. It may not be that he won't love you in the way you long for—but he *can't*. And that is more disappointment. I really do understand. Yet he does love you, in his way. And you him, in your way."

These connections are starting to make sense. "Why," Kate asks Marta, "do I feel almost relieved?"

"You may be starting to accept yourself as you are. And others. With less reactivity. Accepting reality as it is." Maybe she is. "You are looking at things many people spend their whole lives avoiding."

"I feel like I'm getting braver."

"And"—Marta changes her tone—"you may want to give yourself a bit of a break from all of this. Don't let it consume you. Just let it be there. This is deep work."

"Yes."

"We are about out of time, and I want to let you know something." She speaks softly. "I'm considering taking some time off soon."

"You are?" Kate's mouth is suddenly dry. "When?"

"In a month or so."

"Where? How long?"

"Well, my children are both out of college now, and I may just go back to Holland for a while. Live on my houseboat." Marta smiles warmly. "Maybe for nine or ten months, something like that."

"Wow."

Kate's hand rests absentmindedly on her stomach. Along with a sense of dread imagining Marta being gone, she can't help feeling excited for her.

"Maybe I'll do some writing myself," Marta continues. "I've not made up my mind for sure. And either way, we still have several more sessions before then. I just thought it best to mention it now. This wasn't planned, this trip. But the more I think about it, the more I like the idea."

"I'll really miss you. Yet this sounds amazing." Marta's presence, her guidance and compassion, have felt life altering.

"And I'll be back."

"You'd better! I'm not cured yet!"

Marta's laughter fills the room. "This is good work, Kate. Really. Don't rush it. Just sit in the muck for as long as it takes. There's a lot in here, in your life. And in the sadness. The depth of our sorrow can help show us who we are." This feels true. "And when you're ready, I would love to read your writing. You can always send it to me."

"Thank you, Marta. You've helped me start to heal. Just knowing you."

Kate leaves Marta's office feeling a myriad of emotions. Something begins to form in her mind. *The value of sadness . . .* She scrambles through her purse. A piece of paper. Even a scrap. *It is sorrow that has made me . . .* She finds the back of an envelope. And a pen. She sits right on the curb.

My deep sadness has shown me who I am.
Without this,
Without the courage to go
—to fall—
Further than I imagined,
I would be only a shadow of myself.
There is a merging,
An integration,
That can happen between light and dark.
Seen and unseen.
There is a hidden dance

SPLIT OPEN

In that place.
It is sacred.
Cannot be named.
This weaving is my life's work.
My undoing.
Salvation.
On my ninety-ninth birthday,
I hope to look upon the life I've lived
With awe,
Knowing I did more than I ever thought possible.
This work is tucked deep in my soul,
Has become me.
My sorrow has not ruled me with its separateness.
It has crawled into my very core . . .
And learned to shine.

Kate folds the envelope and puts it in her purse. Looking up. Facing the sunshine.

Jennifer

"How about a half hour?"

"Sounds good. Oh, Ana? What are you wearing?"

"Jeans and a top. Sexy casual."

Jennifer can't help laughing. Who says that? "Okay. Thanks. You have my address?"

"I do!" Her voice is bright. "See you soon."

"Bye."

"Bye!"

Sexy casual. This will be her first party as a single woman. There will be artists there. And musicians. Jennifer's stomach does a full flip. Is she ready for this? She moves to her closet, grabbing her black jeans. She always feels good in those. What shirt? She'd better pick something fast.

Jennifer looks down. There, on the ground lies her favorite top with shades of reds, oranges, and pinks. It had fallen off the hanger. She thinks of Ana's final painting. Perfect.

Jennifer puts on mascara and a little blush. Will there be anyone there that she knows? Does she want there to be? Will Ana want to stay long? Maybe she should take her own car. No, she doesn't want to go alone.

A knock. One final look. Earrings. Jennifer grabs her favorite pair of hoops and slides them into her ears as she walks to the front door.

"Hi!"

Ana looks gorgeous. Her hair is down and curly. And she does look absolutely sexy casual.

"Come in!" Jennifer invites. "You look lovely."

"Thanks. So do you. Wow!" Ana looks around. "This is nice. Are those the kids' rooms?"

"Yeah. Small, but they each have their own. That's good for Chloe."

"I really like it. So much. You have such good taste. Great taste!"

"Thanks. I had fun with it."

"Ever thought of decorating?" Ana asks.

"What. Like for real?"

"Yeah. You did all this yourself?"

Jennifer nods.

"Ever study interior design?"

"No." Jennifer laughs. "You're being sweet."

"No, I'm not." Ana looks at Jennifer. "You really should. You have an artist's eye."

Jennifer feels herself beaming. "Really?" Ana is a true artist.

"Yes. And I'm giving you your first job interview."

"What?"

"My roommate's moving out, getting married. She and her fiancé just bought a house. She asked me today if I knew of a decorator. I want to bring her over."

"Here?" Jennifer's heart beats fast.

"Yes, here. You have no idea, do you?"

"What?"

With piercingly kind eyes, she says, "How talented you are."

"I've been a stay-at-home mom for over a decade. No. I don't."

"Sometimes it takes someone else to see it first." Ana smiles. "Can I please tell my roommate about you?" Scary.

"Yes."

"Good. You're a treasure, Jennifer. You really are. All right, let's go. We're fashionably late enough."

As Jennifer grabs her black purse, she quickly scans her living room. She had taken real pride in fixing up the place. Her place. Inexpensively. She actually enjoyed that. It made her more creative. Maybe more creative than she'd realized.

● ● ●

THE PARTY. JENNIFER ENTERS. THE ROOM IS DIMLY LIT. Intimate. She accepts a glass of wine. It's good as it goes down. She feels she's in a dream.

She can't believe her ease. She feels so free. Jennifer tells someone she is the luckiest woman at the party because she is no longer tied to a marriage.

The night feels extraordinary. Full of possibility. Two women whisper in the corner. They glance at Jennifer. Are they talking about her? So what if they are?

Jennifer feels a power begin to move within her. She has survived so much. Has come out the other side. Not only intact.

Transformed.

Someone touches her arm. Ana. She pulls Jennifer into the next room. The music is loud. Furniture has been cleared. Low light. Moving bodies. Jennifer sets her wine on a small table in the corner. She looks to see Ana heading toward the middle of the room, weaving gracefully between people.

Jennifer creates her own path. The spaces Ana found are no longer there. Jennifer glides through the sea of bodies until she finds herself at the center.

She begins to dance.

Epilogue

Dear Marta,

I hope you are enjoying life on your boat.

Here it is. Finished.

You've helped me more than you will ever know. I'm done with Jennifer's story, or perhaps I should say Jennifer is done with me. Whichever the case, her story is complete, and now, finally, I am ready to write my own.

With great gratitude,
Kate

Book Club Discussion Questions

1. Kate and Jennifer seem, at times, to lead parallel lives. If these women got to know one another, how do you think they'd feel about each other? How are they similar and different . . . as mothers? . . . as wives? . . . as women?

2. Who is Jennifer, really? Why do you think the author has chosen to present Jennifer this way?

3. Is Kate happy? When? Is Jennifer happy? When?

4. How do you relate to the character of Kate? Jennifer?

5. Do you think these women's lives and relationships (including their female relationships) are realistic? Why?

6. How do dreams function in this book?

7. What role does creativity play in the lives of female characters? Do you think creativity is different for women than it is for men?

8. This author gives more attention to the bodily sensations of her female and child characters than she does to the bodies of men in this book. Why might this be?

9. What role does age play in these characters' lives?

10. In some ways, Kate and David limit each other. Are these limitations good for each of them, or are they damaging?

11. Is James a different kind of father in the first half of the book than he is in the second?

12. Which scene has stuck with you the most? How did it impact you? Do you think you'll remember it in a few months or years?

13. There's a lot of spirituality and religion referenced in this book—but is there anything that the book suggests is sacred?

14. There are aspects of the plot that could be described as surreal. Why might the author have chosen to make it hard for us to know what's real?

15. If you could recommend this book to anyone, who would you most like to have read it? Why?

Acknowledgments

To my remarkable editor, Kerry Stapley, I offer deep gratitude for your skill, encouragement, and heart. Your guidance brought life and shape to my words. At every turn, you held me in your graceful and capable hands.

Hanna Kjeldbjerg, my amazing project manager, you are all talent, heart, and wisdom—complete with generous hand-holding. Your gentle leadership and care made this leap possible. My affinity and gratitude for you abound. Athena Currier, thank you for capturing the essence of this piece with your radiant and compelling design work. Sara Lynn, thank you for your proofread, attention to detail, and kind feedback. Thanks to Evan Allgood for your careful critical read and to Becca Hart for all you do. Lily Coyle, publisher and owner of The Publishing Pond, thank you. This team of genuine, gifted, strong women midwifed *Split Open* into being with powerful synchronicity.

Thanks to my early readers, Beth Lodge-Rigal, Dortee Farrar, PhD, Dr. Robert Simmermon, Sarah Bell, Cynthia Bretheim, Kay Minniear, DC, Carla Carey, and Sarah Villwock. You gave me the courage to continue.

Thank you to my more recent readers and supporters, John Bailey, Jayme Mattler, Kenton Glick, and especially Cady McClain for your deep belief in me and this narrative.

Thanks to Mary Pierce Brosmer and Women Writing for (a) Change®, as well as Beth Lodge-Rigal and Women Writing for (a) Change®, Bloomington, for creating safe, sacred spaces for words and embodied sharing. To Dortee Farrar, PhD, for your unwavering belief in the value of creative work. To dreamwork with Robert Moss. Heartfelt gratitude to my beloved teachers MaDar Brown and Trikaya Olliffe, and to Love—the greatest teacher of all.

My sweet, longtime friend, Laurie Flanigan-Hegge—*Split Open* would not exist in this form without you. Thank you for connecting me with, and entrusting me to, The Pond. I honor you and our close friends, who always keep it real. Also, thank you Beth Lodge-Rigal for your authentic friendship and support in writing and life.

Thank you to my friend and father of my children, Angelo Pizzo. Thanks to my dear and loving sister, Mary Lind. Also, my brother, Michael Lind. Mom and Dad, thank you for raising and loving me—see you on the flip side!

To the brightest lights, my wonderful sons Anthony and Quinn: I love you with my whole heart. Being your mom is the single greatest gift of my life.

And to you, dear reader.

A SPECIAL THANK YOU TO:

Maresa Murray, PhD
Indiana University
Associate Clinical Professor-Human Development and Family Studies
Director of Undergraduate Studies-Department of Applied Health Science
Assistant Dean of Diversity, Inclusion, and Organizational Climate
School of Public Health-Bloomington

Your holistic racial bias sensitivity read and in-depth consulting helped me see what I could not see myself. Thank you for your focus, knowledge, and generosity, for bringing full voice to Nia, and for helping me be brave within my vulnerability.

)))))